# WILLIWAW
# WINDS

4.1"

# WILLIWAW WINDS

## SALLY BAIR

*Sally Bair*

Cedar Haven Books
Washburn, Wisconsin

The characters and events in this book are fictitious. Any similarity to real persons, living or dead, is coincidental and not intended by the author.

Published by
Cedar Haven Books
P.O. Box 186
Washburn, Wisconsin 54891-0186
cedarhavenbooks@gmail.com

Cover design by Dunn+Associates, www.dunn-design.com
Cover illustration by Roland Dahlquist, rollied@q.com
Interior design by Dorie McClelland, Spring Book Design,
   www.springbookdesign.com
The text of this book is set in Adobe Garamond Pro.

09 10 11 12 13  5 4 3 2 1
*First Edition*

Library of Congress Control Number: 2009908385
ISBN-13: 978-0-9841346-9-4

To the United States Coast Guard
to whom I am forever grateful

For Rudy

# Acknowledgments

My heartfelt thanks—

—to my son, Jarl, whose story of survival gave me the inspiration to write this book. Jarl, I greatly appreciate your generous help in teaching me about the crab fishing industry.

—to the Yarnspinners for their dedication, loving spirit, and relentless help in critiquing *Williwaw Winds*: Mary Jacobson, Boyd Sutton, Carolyn Marquardt, Dorothy Lund, and other former members.

—to my daughter, Cherrie, for her ongoing support and encouragement in all my writing projects.

—to my sisters, Sandy and Jo, for their loving acceptance of me in spite of my foibles and flights of fantasy.

—to my mother who shared her writing genes with me and always knew I'd be a published writer. Mom, if you were still here, you'd be my most loyal cheerleader.

—to Ann, my niece, for her keen, listening ear as I read my stories; Wanda, Dave, Bill, Renee, and Gary of my weekly prayer group who faithfully asked God for His favor on my book; Pastor Ron, whose encouragement, from one writer to another, has kept my spirits high; the Northwest Regional Writers and the Wisconsin Regional Writers Association, for their ongoing support.

—to my God and Savior, Jesus Christ, for gifting me with the ability, wisdom, and perseverance to continue sharing my stories.

# Contents

WILLIWAW
**WINDS**

*Chapter One*

# LEARNING THE ROPES

"Hey, Horn! Get up here on deck pronto."

I throw my journal in my duffel bag, hoist myself out of my bunk, and wobble out to the deck where the cold, bright sunlight of late October meets my eyes. My muscles itch to kick Freddy in the shins for interrupting my writing—and calling me Horn again. But there's little energy or strength left in me after lying on my smelly bunk puking my guts out from seasickness. I'm only now beginning to feel halfway alive again.

"The skipper says to hurry, Horn. We're almost to the fishin' grounds," Freddy tells me and then laughs. "Ya shoulda seen yerself stumblin' outa the bunkroom. I shoulda got some good shots with that fancy camera ya brought along." He grins crookedly, wickedly. "Ya really are a greenhorn. Green around the gills, that is."

Greenhorn or not, I hate the name. Why did I get stuck with a crew mate like him?

The 72-foot *Danny Boy* rolls and my mouth fills with vomit. Why did I ever want this job, anyway? Four days ago I couldn't wait to leave Anchorage. Sick of watching my sister Joanie struggle with pain since her accident, sick of Dad ignoring me except for all the Bible verses he spouted while helping care for Joanie, sick of having to wait until spring to enroll at the University, I jumped at this chance-in-a-million to go crab fishing. Dad was so preoccupied with Joanie, he had no argument against my leaving, even though I'm only sixteen. Mom's protest was weak, too. I figure they both wanted me out of the way. Now I wonder if the situation at home was as bad as this.

Freddy interrupts my thoughts with another command. All I hear is the word Horn. I grind my teeth.

"My name's Jacob Bergren, remember? Call me Jake, not Horn." There's a sneer in my voice but I don't care. "You're a jerk, Freddy Schumaker! What do you have against me anyway?"

Freddy's face turns red as a squalling baby. He balls his fists, gets right in my face. "Ya stupid city brat, ya stole my . . . aw, what's the diff? Too late anyway." And he walks away.

Stunned, confused, I don't dare go after him. Someday I'll learn the truth about Freddy's hostility.

Staring out from portside, I focus on the horizon. There's a blur of land in the far distance.

"Hey! I thought we were in the middle of the Bering Sea. What's that piece of land doing out here?" In my surprise, I've forgotten my anger.

"That's St. Paul Island. I told ya before, that's where

we pick up our crab pots and bait . . . but come on. Skipper says I hafta show ya the ropes on board. Now that yer among the livin' again." Freddy looks down at a mass of tangled lines next to me. "'Course ya don't wanna be trippin' over any of *them* ropes."

Freddy jabs me hard in my side. So hard, I reel. My head boils. Maybe I do have enough energy to kick him.

But he must read my mind because he steps back quickly and then leers at me. "Be nice, Horn. After all, yer dad bein' a chaplain and all. Wouldn't want him to spank you, would ya?"

My face heats up. Why is this guy tormenting me?

"Yer just a punk kid, that's why. Even if ya are bulked up."

He's got to be psychic. Just because I'm still sixteen— but not for long—he calls me a punk kid? After the award I won for high school wrestling? Seems longer than just last year, but I'm still in good shape. I can beat the skinny pants off Freddy. Hands down, soon as I regain my strength. I just hope he never learns that the kids at school called me Beef. It's almost as bad as Horn.

Freddy holds up a hand. "Don't try nothin', Horn. Yer too weak." He spits out his freaky laugh.

I lunge at him just as a wave rolls the boat and I trip over a piece of line the same color as the deck. Next thing I know, I'm flat on my back looking at the winter-bright sky. Anger whooshes out of me like a spouting whale. My hand finds the lower deck rail.

"Be careful by the rail, Horn," Freddy warns. "Don'tcha know every year some guys get swept overboard?" He points to Marv, another crewman. "Marv's brother was one of 'em. That reminds me, Horn. Don't ever go out on deck without the knife in yer knife belt. It'll give ya a fightin' chance ta get free if ya tangle in the lines and get washed overboard when the seas flood the deck."

While I pat the knife belt attached to my rain coat, Freddy's wild cackle echoes the length of the *Danny Boy*.

Marv and Patrick, the other crewmen, look up from their tasks and shake their heads. Good thing the skipper, Ron McIntosh, is in the wheelhouse. Wouldn't want him to see me like this. Don't want him to think I'm too much of a klutz to help the crew fish for hair crabs. I'm determined to learn the ropes of crab fishing in a more dignified manner, so I take a deep breath and untangle myself. With a snort of laughter, Freddy offers me a hand up.

Heading for St. Paul, which I learned in school is one of the Pribilof Islands, the boat bounces over six- to eight-foot waves. Will my tender stomach be able to take this for five more weeks?

"Lord, give me strength," I whisper.

"Let's get this show on the road, Horn," Freddy says. Then he mutters to himself. "Don't see why I hafta be the one to show a punk kid the ropes. There oughta be a law 'gainst babies being hired on Bering Sea crab boats.

Not fair. Shoulda been Pete, my . . . why can't Patrick, the whiz kid, show him around?"

If looks could kill, I'd be a dead fish.

Who's Pete? I wonder. And what's Freddy's grudge with Patrick?

In an instant, Freddy's all business. "See the tower above ya?" He points to a long, slender pole near the wheelhouse. "That's the mast. The winch that's hooked to it lifts our anchors on board an' the hydraulic block pulls our fishin' lines in. By the way, do ya know the difference between starboard and port?"

I roll my eyes. "Any dummy knows starboard is on the right side of a boat and port on the left. And the stern's in the back."

Freddy grins. "Jist checkin', Horn, jist checkin'."

I don't know everything, though, and find the big machinery around me amazing. Will I ever learn how it all works? Some of it sits near the stern, which rides lower in the water than lots of other boats I've seen. I picture cold waves washing over the deck.

"Soon we'll be fishin', Horn. And makin' money. Ya gonna be ready?" Freddy rubs his hands together, glee spreading all over his face.

His quick changes of mood puzzle me. But like him, I find the money part exciting. At least we have something in common.

An unusually big wave rolls the boat. Lurching, I reach for the rail, forgetting Freddy's warning. He grabs my rain jacket and wrenches me away. I gasp at the speed of his grip and before my first full breath, he yells at me.

"How stupid can ya get, Horn? Tryin' to kill yerself?" Freddy's anger washes over the boat just like that wave, drawing stares from the others. I feel lower than a seal crawling over the harbor rocks.

What have I got myself into? A bouncing boat that matches my bouncing stomach? A jerk to work with? All because I want to make some quick money for college? All because I can't stand watching Joanie suffer? Joanie's a year younger than I am. She was hurt in a hit-and-run accident last May and ended up in a wheelchair and in a lot of pain. She and my parents believe she'll walk again. Me—I don't believe in miracles any more. I did my share of praying for Joanie's recovery but nothing came of it. I even missed fall semester at the university because of her.

Yanking my thoughts back to the boat, I look above the wheelhouse at the four-foot-wide radio and radar antennas swaying in the wind. Flimsy and fragile look-ing, they turn in a sweeping motion. How reliable are they in a storm? Except for them, we'd be all alone out here. The thought makes me shiver.

"That's our only communication between the *Danny Boy* and land," Freddy explains. "Them instruments'll come in handy when a williwaw hits us."

"A what?" So what's he scaring me about now? I narrow my eyes into angry slits as he flashes his freaky smile again. How my fingers itch to throw him overboard. Aaugh!

"Don'tcha know what a williwaw is? When the wind blows off the Bering Sea, it picks up speed when it hits the mountains along the Alaska Peninsula. We passed 'em on the way out but you were down below, pukin' and stinkin' up the bunkroom. Anyway, the winds turn nasty. Violent, even. A hundred knots sometimes, when they hit the sea. They make the sea boil. Come on fast. One gust after another. Them's called williwaws. Bein' a chaplain's son, ya better pray we don't get caught in any williwaws."

Shivers travel down my body again. The Bering Sea is rolling hard enough now, in my estimation; I can't imagine being in a williwaw. Would God even help us get out of one? Why should He care? He didn't help Joanie. Can I count on Him for anything?

Freddy points to the row of large floodlights mounted to the mast. "We use 'em when we work at night, Horn."

"Hey! No one told me we work at night. When do we sleep?"

"Sleep? Ha! Like I told ya, ya'll have a hard time keepin' up, Horn . . . let's go up and see the skipper . . . and yes, we did tell ya about working' at night. Ya jist fergot."

Freddy leads me upstairs to show me the wheelhouse where the skipper is manning the controls. I already know him from when I got this job.

Between the constant engine hum and the wind, it's a noisy place. The whole boat is, for that matter.

Windows nearly surround the wheelhouse. I gaze at the mesmerizing ocean waves outside every window. From up here they look twice as big as they are. Like a rollercoaster, the boat rolls up one wave and plunges down the other side into a deep trough. Every high point gives me a clear view of St. Paul off in the distance. The skipper must have an iron stomach to stay up here hour after day after week.

This is my first time up here. When we left Homer four days ago, I spent my time watching at the rail while we motored across calm, Kachemak Bay. But my stomach started to churn once we headed into the open sea. That was the end of me on deck until this morning. And if I stay here much longer, I may end up in my bunk again. Pulling my gaze away from the windows, I listen to Freddy and the skipper talk about the weather.

"Have you shown Jake everything on the boat yet?" The skipper asks Freddy.

"Not yet. Guess we'd better be goin'," Freddy tells me.

We head for the work deck where Freddy points to two huge, steel hatch covers on the floor. One is full and overflowing with water.

"These are the fish holds. We dump the hair crabs in 'em when we pull our pots."

I peer through a round hole in the cover of the empty hold. It looks bottomless.

"Spooky, huh?" Freddy's ghoulish grin reminds me of Frankenstein's monster.

"How deep are they?" I ask.

"'Bout nine feet. They hold about fifty thousand pounds of crabs. Ya can't fall in through the hole, but ya could trip on a cover and break an ankle. Gotta be careful on deck."

Freddy's warning sounds out of character. Is he actually being nice to me? Or did the skipper make his warnings part of my tour? At any rate, he finishes the tour so I go back to the fo'c'sle—that means "forward castle"—where my bunk is waiting. On the same level as the deck is also the galley, which is the kitchen, and the head, what I call the bathroom.

In the galley, fluorescent lights shine down on a washer and dryer, an electric stove, a fridge, and a table bolted to the floor. Bags and boxes of groceries are stored everywhere—our food for the trip. The shelves can't hold it all. For the first time since we hit the open sea, I feel hungry and wonder what's in the boxes. Something good, I hope.

A door near the galley leads to a steep, steel stairway. Freddy sneaks in behind me.

"Fergot ta show ya the engine room, Horn. Come on."

He leads the way down and opens the door. The engine noise and smell of diesel fuel overpower me. Swallowing to keep down the saliva, I lose the battle and gag.

Freddy snorts, socks me on the arm. "Knew ya couldn't take it, Horn."

I make a run for the head and then stagger back to my bunk, a familiar, vile taste filling my mouth. It won't leave. Neither will the smell in my nostrils, which matches that of the blanket under me. I look around. The bunkroom is dark, cramped, and messy. Not a bit neat like I like things. These guys are slobs just like Joanie used to be. I wince, picturing her stuck in that wheelchair. What I'd give to see her room in a mess again, but Mom keeps it so neat now it doesn't seem like Joanie's any more.

Freddy leaves me alone so I can finish writing in my journal. It's Joanie's journal, really. At least I'm dedicating it to her since she gave it to me as an early Christmas gift so I can write about this trip.

I run my hands over the smooth, red leather cover, still amazed that Joanie gave me this unique gift. It's a nautical log book with sixty-pound paper that feels as heavy as the sketch pad pages she uses for her art projects.

"It's not waterproof," she told me when she handed it to me, "but it won't get soggy or fall apart in the humid sea air."

I pick up the waterproof pen she also gave me, and write.

*This fishing trip sucks, Joanie. It's a long ways from here to Anchorage. I could have used a doctor the last few days. About died of seasickness. And this seventy-two-foot tub creep-*

*ing along at ten miles an hour—oops, I mean about eight knots, since a knot equals one-point-one-four mph—up and down and up and down the ocean troughs. It's no picnic.*

*There's nothing to see out here but water and sky and a little island. And a jerk named Freddy who uses terrible grammar. And he has a weird scar on his upper lip. Hard to tell when he smiles and when he sneers. It's easy to figure what side of the tracks he comes from. He's twenty but looks forty. His black hair hangs in a greasy ponytail. He's not as bulked up as I am so I think I can take him easily. It's tempting because he won't get off my back. He persists in dogging me—follows me everywhere. I feel trapped on this twenty-two-foot-wide tub.*

*But I try to keep the peace . . .*

Well, not really.

*. . . and follow all the rules.*

That's a lie, too. No fighting aboard ship, the skipper said my first day on. And here I am ready to do a half Nelson on Freddy.

*I admit, he's teaching me stuff about the boat I didn't know. Like a fathom is six feet. Rigging consists of the boom, and the mast with its long arms and lines attached.*

*Freddy's talk about our possible earnings—our share, it's called—has me excited. He says some guys make twenty thousand bucks a trip. I'll be happy with less than half that. All the guys act like they have the gambling fever.*

*By the way, how's The Terminator? It's hard to believe you'd actually give your wheelchair such a name. Like you know for sure that its use will be terminated because you'll walk on your own some day.*

*Are Mom and Dad lonesome for me? Ha. Not after me grumbling about missing out on fall term in college. Not that it's your fault, Joanie. Wasn't your fault some s.o.b. messed you up.*

*Sure was nice of them to give me my Christmas gift early, though. Who wouldn't be pleased with an eight-pixel, digital camera? I promise to take lots of pix for you.*

*Put in a good word for me in your prayers, Joanie. After all, you're still on God's side and I'm not. Not after what happened to you.*

*Sorry for leaving you on bad terms. I didn't mean those nasty words about your faith in God. Glad you find your peace in him. Let's agree to disagree, okay?*

I stuff my journal and pen in the duffel and close my eyes. Can I let Joanie read this? Maybe I'll censor it with a black marker before giving it to her.

I doze, dreaming of Joanie wrestling with me on our lawn and playing touch football like we did before the accident. Dreaming of all the money I'll make on this fishing trip. Enough for second semester so Dad won't have to help. I can make it on my own. Without his help. Without God's help. God helps those who help themselves, people say. I don't remember reading it in my Bible, though. Hmm.

If only we can get this slow, ten-mile-an-hour . . . I mean eight-knots . . . trip over with.

*Chapter 2*

# ST. PAUL ISLAND

It's still daylight when a storm kicks up as we approach St. Paul Island. The wind sounds like a banshee, waking me up. My stomach turns queasy again. Maybe Freddy is right; maybe I'll do better on deck than in bed. Keep looking at the horizon, he told me.

In a wink it turns calm. I sit up when a hard jerk of the boat nearly throws me off the bunk. What did we hit? I rush out to the deck, surprised and thankful the *Danny Boy* is banging against a long, wooden pier and being tied to the cannery dock. I'm amazed at the stacks of crab pots lining the dock. All sizes and shapes.

The storm rages out beyond the harbor. I'm glad we're protected.

Stepping off the *Danny Boy* onto the St. Paul Island dock, the crew doesn't waste any time. Each man grabs a pot from our boat's stack of a thousand and checks it over. The crewmen of several other boats are also working on their own gear.

Our pots—designed especially for hair crabs—are about thirty inches across and weigh fifteen pounds.

Each has a steel ring on the bottom, covered with nylon mesh. PVC braces support the pots upward to their funnel-like top. The PVC supports are surrounded by nylon webbing which is stretched and tied shut.

"Come on, Horn, start checkin' these pots." Freddy gives me a stern nod.

The guys are patching holes in the webbing with nylon line. Freddy beckons me over.

"All of these bios need replacin'," he says.

"What's a bio?" I ask. I watch him closely as he works on a pot.

"See how the webbing is slit here?" Freddy points to a long, horizontal opening just above the bottom ring. "It's the bio. We patch the hole with cotton twine. We hafta do it. Gov'ment says so. Fer the envir'ment. See, if a pot is lost from its line and there's a crab in it, the cotton twine will dissolve—I mean biodegrade—so the crab can get out. Nylon webbing won't dissolve so we hafta add these cotton patches. Wouldn't want the crabs to die that way, would we?" Freddy winks, but a look of disgust crosses his face. "A big headache, if ya ask me. But no one's askin'."

I smile. "But it's the law, right? I get it."

The others grin while they work alongside us. Marv keeps watching me. His eyes look sinister. Funny I haven't noticed him watching me before. Should I be afraid of him?

We patch holes and tie twine for hours while taking

turns transferring stacks of ten or fifteen repaired pots to the deck with the hydraulic lift. We keep working well into the night.

The wind howls outside the harbor.

"We're in for a good blow, boys," the skipper tells us. "Good timing for it. We can keep working while we wait out the storm. Go get some sleep. A couple more days of this and maybe we can start fishing."

Sleep comes fast after I hit my bunk. It's still dark when Patrick shakes me awake the next morning for the walk we'd planned last night.

"Are you ready? We have a couple hours before gear work. Meet me on deck in five minutes. And dress warm. We'll be facing the wind some."

"You bet I'm ready. Anything to be on land for awhile."

I dress in layers of shirts and long johns and sweatpants, wool socks, and a tight, wool hat pulled over my ears. Everything but my rain gear. I pull my new camera out of the duffel and in seconds I'm ready. The harbor is fairly calm but outside the seawall huge breakers crash against the rocks.

We step off the boat and start walking through the town of St. Paul. Not much to see—a store, a bar, a church, the cannery, a school, and a post office for the five hundred or so people who live here. There's a Coast Guard base, too, and a National Weather Service station. I can't imagine working on this desolate island, let alone living here in the wind that rarely quits.

A few seals sun themselves on the rocky, harbor shore. Others wriggle into the water and dive as a big wave comes in. When they come out of a dive, their heads pop up, long whiskers making them look like old men bobbing in the waves. The seals are big. Bigger than my Lab-retriever.

I watch for awhile and then confront Patrick. I have to know. "So what's with Freddy, anyway? Why has he got it in for me?"

Patrick sighs. "Didn't anybody tell you? You got the job Freddy's cousin, Pete, was supposed to have. Guess he's sore about that. But Freddy's not a bad guy. He always teases the horns when they come on board. He's feisty sometimes, but that's because he's had to fight his way up in this world. His dad left the family, you know. And his mom has had to work two jobs to support the kids and maintain their little trailer on the outskirts of town. Freddy works hard to help her out. He's really a good guy. He held the bucket for you when you were seasick, you know."

"I don't believe it."

But Patrick nods. "You were really out of your head those days."

I don't want to hear about Freddy helping me. "So what's with his scar?" I ask.

"Oh, that. I'm so used to it I forget he had surgery for a cleft lip years ago. Some call it a hair-lip. Anyway, kids were mean to him. He eventually quit school over it but he's a survivor. Got a heart as big as the Bering Sea. Don't let him scare you, especially about hair crab fishing. It's a lot safer than going for the king crabs, or the opilios which are called snow crabs. Those fishermen go out in January, during the colder and stormier season. Their gear is much bigger and heavier. Much harder work, much more dangerous." Patrick stops walking. "My dad's boat is safe. He's a careful skipper."

His words reassure me. Maybe it won't be so bad after all.

"Ever been here before?" Patrick asks and continues talking. "Those are Northern fur seals you see, all females. There aren't many that hang around this time of year, but we'll be seeing some bulls on our walk."

Boy, have I been missing out. I've lived in Anchorage for three years but have so much more to see in Alaska. Guess I've been spending too much time in the gym.

"The Pribilof Islands were discovered by a Russian guy, Gavriil Pribilof. Bet you didn't know that. Lots of people don't. By the way, the Pribilof Islands are volcanic."

I can tell Patrick's planning to go on with his history lesson so I say nothing as we walk across the tundra toward the beach outside of town.

"We're on the Bering Sea Shelf," he continues. "It's the main force of the economy in the Bering Sea. Crab fishing is a hugely profitable business here. The shallower waters go out about ten miles or so before they drop off into the Aleutian Basin. The basin is called the

Greenbelt because phytoplankton constantly flows up the slope and mixes with the shallower, shelf waters."

I laugh. "Wow, you're a walking encyclopedia. By the way, do the king crabs live in the deeper waters?" I ask.

"Kings, yes, and tanners, and Bristol Bay salmon, and other species. Opilios are the most sought after by fishermen."

I clear my throat. "So how do we catch hair crabs, anyway? With hair nets?"

He laughs. "That sounds like Freddy's type of humor. You taking after him?"

I shake my head. "No way!"

Before I can say another word, Patrick spouts off more history.

"Pribilof discovered the fur seal rookeries in 1788. In 1867 the islands and Alaska were passed to the United States. The fur seals were so over-harvested that in 1966 it became forbidden to hunt them, except for subsistence hunting by the natives."

"You mean the Aleuts?"

"And the Indians and Eskimos," Patrick adds.

Out of the corner of my eye I catch a small movement across the dusting of snow.

"Is that a fox?" I ask. The creature is bluish-brown in color and has a thick coat of fur. I capture him in my zoom lens. Joanie will love it.

"Yes, an Arctic fox. There are hundreds on the island. Soon they'll turn lighter in color, almost white, to blend in with the snow and ice. Right now they're at the end of their summer blue phase. Believe it or not, St. Paul Island is a popular tourist area in the summer. Nature lovers come by the droves, including birders," Patrick continues. "This area is a bird-watcher's paradise with about twenty million seabirds that breed here. Nearly two hundred fifty species—can you believe it? The tufted puffin, albatross, spectacled eider—they're so neat—and kittiwake. Those are kittiwakes flying over there." He points to a small flock out over the water. "We're headed for Ridge Wall, the high cliff where tour buses take visitors in the summer. Just wait till you see the bull fur seals. They're awesome."

"Do people fish here in the summer? Or only in winter like we are?" I ask.

"Halibut fishing is big in the summer. So are cod and pollock fishing. And scientists come by the dozens. It's a busy place, nothing like now." Patrick turns my way and grins. "You should come in the summer. You'd see thousands of fur seals. Many of them follow the small tour buses for handouts."

Our walk on the windward side of St. Paul toward the cliff brings a constant roar. Which is louder, wind or waves? I can't tell. My ears are assaulted even through my heavy, wool cap.

We must have walked a mile by now along the already-snow-covered, rolling hills. I can picture the landscape full of colorful, summer wildflowers. Makes me wonder why I'm here now, why I don't wait for summer to fish for halibut instead.

I gasp for breath as we approach the cliff edge. Breakers roll in with relentless regularity. The rocky beach is scattered with noisy, smelly fur seals—all bulls. Their low barks compete with the noise of wind and waves.

"You should hear these guys in the summer. They bellow like trumpets and always stay here on the windiest part of the island. The females stay in the lee with their pups. They're black and cute as a sailor's buttons."

"Ever see any whales?" I ask.

"Definitely. I've seen pods of gray whales and humpbacks, even bowheads when they're migrating. The rarest whale in the world is the North Pacific right whale. I hope to see one someday. I've seen belugas and orcas, too, and plenty of walruses and sea lions. On our halibut trips that take us way out past the Pribilofs, I always see some."

Patrick's history lesson goes on while I watch the bull seals and fill my camera lens with good action shots. The light is perfect for photos. What a riot the seals are. They climb far up the rocky shore and, when a big wave comes in, dive into the heavy surf. Long seconds later, their heads pop up about three hundred yards out. Patrick says they dive for all kinds of fish and for squid, their main diet.

The air here is different from that in the open ocean.

The pungent odor of fur seals, mixed with salty, wind-blown sea spray, almost makes my nose burn. It's not obnoxious, just different.

Patrick and I stand in the wind watching the bulls plunge into the sea and then crawl out—like kids playing on a warm beach. We eventually start back.

I think about Patrick's comments. This is an awesome place and Patrick's input helps make it more so.

"Now I know why Freddy calls you a whiz kid," I tell him. "So how come you never went to college?"

Patrick stops, kicks the snow with his boot. His face clouds over before he starts walking again.

"I was planning to go. I want to be a marine biologist some day. But I started fishing for Dad and really like it. Dad wants me to get my degree, but since Mom almost died in the hospital, I . . . I just feel the need to stay close to Dad. What if something would happen to him, too? Weird, huh? I . . . never mind." A sheepish smile crosses Patrick's face as he gazes at the ground.

We reach the edge of town in silence as I ponder this info. What's Patrick hiding? Is he a wimp, or a mental case? And what about Freddy? Is he "really a good guy"? Maybe he is, but maybe I should watch my back. Guess I've grown cynical since Joanie's accident. If I can't trust God, who can I trust?

I pull my thoughts away from Freddy and ask, "So how's your mom these days?"

A wide smile stretches across Patrick's face. "Doing great. We're sure grateful for your dad's prayers when she was in the hospital. Without them, she might not still be with us. It was a miracle."

I let out a snort. A miracle? Yeah, right. Where was God when Joanie needed Him?

"The 'miracle' is that I got this job," I say with sarcasm.

"Yeah, I'd sure call it that, Jake. How else would you have gotten a job like this at age sixteen? It's unheard of. I'm just surprised your dad even let you take it."

I snort again. "Only because he's so wrapped up in Joanie's care, that's why." Without explaining, I switch gears. "You don't look a bit like your dad," I say. "He's so skinny and you're . . . not fat, but . . . well, chunky."

Patrick's laugh is as big as he is. "You're no Skinny Sam yourself. Guess I got my mom's genes. And the red hair like Dad's dad." He adds seriously, "But not the temper that goes with it. Just want you to know."

I join in his laughter as we approach the *Danny Boy*.

Back on deck, I look out beyond the breakwater. We're a million miles from nowhere. There's work ahead, and potential danger with this winter crab fishing in the Bering Sea. Especially the danger of williwaws between here and home.

We start repairing pots again, working all day and long into the night, the wind still blowing at gale force. I'm getting half the sleep I'm used to. And this trip is just beginning. After two more days and nights, we finally finish the job. And the winds have finally gone down some.

"Let's get this show on the road, boys," the skipper shouts. "It's a nice morning to catch crabs."

# Chapter 3

# SETTING GEAR

Weather is good and excitement is high as we leave St. Paul. A new man boards the *Danny Boy* with us.

"Jake, meet Erickson, our observer," Patrick says.

Observer? As in watching us work? I wonder.

Erickson grasps my hand in a hard grip. "Glad to meet you. In case you're wondering, I won't be breathing down your neck. My job is to collect data on the number of crabs you guys catch, and stuff like that."

"Yeah, and he gets to quit after eight hours a day," Freddy says. "Ya'll catch him readin' or sleepin' in the galley most of his off-time while we bust our butts."

Erickson laughs. "You know how it is with us government workers."

Freddy jabs him in the arm. "Aw, he's a good guy, Horn. Even takes his turn at galley duty cookin' and washin' dishes."

"Sounds like you've worked with this crew before," I say.

"Enough times so I can tell you which guys to look out for." He winks and laughs again.

"Actually, he does have a serious job," Patrick tells me. "He has to keep track of the number of pots we pull and how much soaking time we give the pots. He collects samples of the bycatch . . . you know, other things we catch. Like octopuses and starfish. He'll be on board until we drop off our last load of crabs."

While we talk, Marv runs the hydraulic boom to load four pallets of cardboard boxes filled with frozen bait. The skipper already has the engines warming up. Time to say goodbye to good old terra firma. I shrug into my two-piece, orange rain gear and XTRATUF™, neoprene boots that will keep me from slipping on the wet deck.

We lift the forty-pound boxes, placing half of them in our walk-in freezer and the rest under the long work table. By now the deck is so full, there's barely room to walk.

Freddy glances my way. "Better learn quick how to set gear, Horn. We use two thousand pounds o' bait a day, if yer askin'."

I'm not, but I'm impressed—and discouraged. I'd rather be working out for a wrestling match than this.

While motoring out to the fishing grounds, we fill bait jars. My required knife feels secure on my belt as I fill the hopper of our huge grinder, one box of bait at a time, while Marv operates the controls. The frozen herring and cod are pulverized and it's pooped out of the grinder opening into a large crate. Ugh! I never did like the smell of fish.

"Okay, Horn. Watch how I do this," Freddy says.

As I empty boxes into the hopper, he dips a gloved hand into a smelly crate. He slaps the gray, slimy goop into a bait jar, a half-gallon plastic bottle with a wide mouth.

"See these holes?" Freddy points to the dozens of holes around the jar. "Them's what bring the fish smell to the crabs." He throws the jar into a crab pot.

This'll be a piece of cake. Freddy, Patrick, and I kneel on the deck and fill jars and transfer them to the crab pots as fast as we can while Marv operates the grinder. It's dirty, stinky work. Soon I'm sweating and greasy fish guts are glued to my rain gear and gloves. And boots. And hat. I shudder. Not such a piece of cake after all.

Marv's gaze follows me everywhere. But unlike Freddy, he's quiet. Spooky quiet.

Freddy watches me too, and laughs. "Knew ya wouldn't like it, Horn. Bet ya'd rather be wrestlin' a man instead of bait, huh?" He turns aside with a snort.

The others grin. Embarrassed, I taste bitter anger, grit my teeth. Freddy knows me too well. One of these times—soon as I regain my strength—I'll get even with him.

I reach for another handful of bait, fill a jar, and cover it. Reach, fill, cover. Reach, fill, cover. Over and over. Hour after hour. I'm tired. My knees hurt. My hands sting from the cold and from the salty fish goop that seeps through my glove openings. My stomach churns.

How can these guys joke around while doing this stinky, tiring, mind-numbing job? What I'd give to be out of here. But I'm trapped.

"Come on, Jake," the skipper yells from the wheel-house over the loud hailer—the speaker that's equipped with a microphone. "Smile. You'll soon be raking in money for college."

Uh-oh. Guess my bad attitude shows on my face.

"Yeah, told ya that ya couldn't stand the pace. This is nothin' ta complain about. Wait till the weather turns and it goes below zero with seas washin' the deck while yer settin' gear." Freddy sticks a handful of herring to my nose.

"Okay, that's it. You're in for it now, freaky Freddy!" I try for a body slam into his skinny frame.

But he's too quick. He jerks back, grabs my hair, and stomps on my foot. Where did he learn these moves? I'm the wrestler, not him!

"Don't call me freaky, Horn! I can take a tackle, but not that." With a mighty shove of his hands, Freddy flattens me.

As I start to get up, the skipper makes a beeline down to the deck. Before I take my next breath, he's grabbing me and Freddy by the front of our raincoats. "Cool down. Both of you. Or you'll never fish for me again. Hear? You know the rules. No drugs, no drinking, no fights."

I skulk back to the task. The skipper squeezes between us as we continue working. Freddy's violent reaction startles me. He's stronger than he looks. Better think twice before I decide to tangle with him again. It might be a losing proposition.

I sneak a scowling glance at Freddy, who's sneaking one back at me. With a wide grin, he winks and turns back to his task. Huh? How can he change so fast from Frankenstein's monster to Mr. Cool? Suddenly my anger dissolves. My mouth turns up a little bit and the skipper returns to the wheelhouse.

When I'm about to fall over from exhaustion, we finish just at dawn. We've worked all night. The sun rises late here in early November, so the lights are still on, shining on the work table. I stagger to my bunk and fall asleep.

Awhile later something wakes me up. Freddy plunks down on the bunk opposite mine. He shares a drag of a cigarette. But it's not cigarette smoke I smell. The sweet, acrid smell of marijuana wafts toward me. With a jerk I sit straight up, bumping my head on the bunk above.

Freddy's low chuckle fills the shadowy room. He holds his weed straight out toward me. "Wanna hit, Horn?"

"You crazy? Want to get caught?"

Freddy laughs again. "Naw, the skipper won't do nothin'. Rules or not. He needs me too much. Chill out, Horn. A hit o' this'll calm yer pukey guts. Whadaya say?"

I lie back down, thinking about my touchy stomach and about my nerves. And about the one time I tried smoking pot. Guess I was eleven when Dad caught me and my friend sharing a joint one day behind the house. He put the fear of Jesus in both of us. Never again, I vowed. But Dad isn't here now and I need some kind of fix. Do I dare?

I catch myself. Dad would be disappointed if he found out. And I'm sure the skipper would tell Dad if he caught me. But how disappointed would God be?

I can just hear Dad. "Jacob, when you wrestle with God, be sure to wrestle for the blessing, not the curse." Funny how he named me Jacob, the Old Testament guy who wrestled with God, and I actually became a wrestler. Did Dad plan it that way? Did God?

"Thanks, Freddy, but no thanks. Can't do it." I look him straight in the eyes.

Freddy throws his hands up. "Just wait till we get caught in them williwaws goin' home. Don't say I didn't warn ya, Horn."

Surprisingly, he puts out his joint and leaves the room. I let out my breath and relax. Wrestling with God for a curse—I sure came close.

Too restless to sleep, I walk out to the deck, camera in hand. Now's my chance to get some shots of the rolling waves and the guys working. I hurry because the others are getting ready to set the crab pots.

Forgetting Freddy's former warning, I lean over the deck to catch a shot of a foam-tipped wave. The boat lurches and, whoosh! My camera flies out of my hand, arcs through the air, and goes down . . . down into the sea. I'm horrified. It could have been me. Chills run up my back. I punch the railing, tears threatening to spill.

Freddy's not going to let me forget. He'll be on my tail the whole trip. Will I be able to stand up to his constant jibes? Can I ever forgive myself?

I know the guys all saw it happen but no one says a word. No one smiles. Not even Freddy.

He clears his throat and turns to me. "Ready to start settin' gear, Horn? We'll set about two hundred pots on a string. That makes five lines, each about a mile long. See the loops here?"

I swipe my eyes and then follow Freddy's finger as he points to loops spaced about every thirty feet down the line. Patrick has already made sure the lines are coiled without tangles and each loop is hooked with a pin.

"We hook a pot on each loop. Gotta keep up, Horn. It's fast work. Watch."

Freddy, standing at the stern, starts the process. It's a complicated chore involving bright orange buoys, nylon sinking line, colored floating line, and anchors. He attaches three inflatable buoys to a hundred fifty feet of the sinking line that feeds out and is tied to the same amount of floating line, which prevents tangling with the anchor. Then the anchor, eight or nine feet of chain links—five hundred pounds worth—keeps the pots on the bottom of the sea. He draws the first line out, one loop at a time, from its coil. He holds a loop open so Marv can hook a pot onto it and let it off the stern.

The two hundred pots are set out, one every thirty feet, and the anchor, floating line, sinking line, buoy process is repeated. The line ends up in a mile-long string of pots. And that's just one line.

My job on the assembly line for now is to lift the pots that Marv throws at my feet and snap them to the loops. He throws the pots from their stacks, one at a time, but too fast. At first, the fifteen-pound, silver pots seem light. But within minutes my arms grow heavy. I feel myself slowing down.

"Horn! Pick up the pace," Marv yells as a loop goes out empty.

"Then slow down," I yell back.

But it's the skipper who's in a hurry, Marv tells me. I've got to keep up.

"The pots remind me of miniature igloos," I share breathlessly with anyone who'll listen.

Everyone laughs.

The thirty-foot length between loops seems long, but when the line slides past my feet as fast as it does, I can see how some loops can go out without a pot. If that isn't bad enough, every time a big swell lifts the *Danny Boy*, the loops go out quicker than I can snap a pot on and even more pots are missed.

The skipper calls down to me from the wheelhouse. I know he can't see me, but he must sense what I'm doing.

"You'll get used to it, Jake," he says over the loud hailer.

I accept his kind words gratefully, but still have to speed up. Got to earn my stripes on this trip. Arms aching, hands burning even with gloves on, I snap pots forever. But finally we finish the first line. One down. Yeah!

In another half hour we'll set the second line. The half hour allows us to travel a distance between lines so they won't tangle in the wind-blown, tide-shifting sea. It also gives us the chance to grab a quick snack.

As we start on the second line, Freddy yells at me from across the deck. "Horn! Yer muscles in shock yet?" He grins crookedly while throwing pots down to Patrick. "Ya shoulda been liftin' yer dumbbells 'steada pukin' in the bunk. Ya wouldn't be so weak."

How does he know I brought my dumbbells? Has he been snooping in my duffel?

He's right, though. My muscles are in shock. My shoulders, my knees, my back. And I'm breathless from the fast pace. Did I lose so much muscle tone from just four days in bed? At least I can rotate jobs with the crew. Throwing pots is the pits.

The work is monotonous. And hard. Tired as I am though, I'm mesmerized watching each pot go off the stern. I picture the pots bouncing along on the uneven, bumpy ocean floor. How deep do they go down, anyway?

"It's about forty fathoms deep here—that's two hundred forty feet fer ya landlubbers," Freddy shouts at me.

He reads my mind again. Freaky.

At last we finish setting the fifth line. Looking back,

I can barely see the buoys as they bob up and down on the sea. In the early dusk, a dozen or more lighted boats are scattered around us, some a mile away.

"Nine hours we've been doing this," the skipper says. "Time for another break. You boys grab a bite while I run us back to the first set so we can start hauling gear."

I don't know if I'm more tired or hungry. The skipper clasps my shoulder with one hand, Freddy's with the other. "Like a well-oiled machine we are," he says. His thin face beams. "Good job, Jake."

We take turns microwaving some frozen burritos. I grab a handful of candy bars, fill my cup with fresh coffee, and sit.

Ah, the hard bench feels good. My arms are limp, straining to bring food to my mouth. Seems like seconds later when the others leave to go back. Mechanically, my feet move forward. No one else moves as slowly as I do. My back muscles scream but I feel good being part of the team. The skipper's right. We work together like a well-oiled machine.

The weather is fair, winds calmer. That means I don't have to strain my overworked muscles while clinging to the table as the boat rocks. Winds measure about twenty knots—a light breeze by crab fishing standards. A larger-than-usual wave hits us occasionally, to maybe twelve feet instead of the usual eight to ten.

Every time a larger wave hits, Patrick cringes. His

dad moves in close to him. He's getting more and more paranoid.

I'm thankful for a stronger stomach. Inside and out, I feel good despite my fatigue. Inside and out, I smile. Freddy glances at me and ruins my mood.

"Just wait, Horn. Ya ain't seen no williwaws yet."

Oh, how I'd love to take out his lights with a gut-buster drop. But recalling the words of my wrestling coach, I tell myself, "Focus, Jake. Don't let anything get to you."

Dad's words click in my brain, too. "Jake, remember Paul's words. 'I can do all things through Christ who strengthens me.' You can do it."

Where that thought came from, I don't even want to guess. Right now I'm not concerned. Not about the wind blowing or about williwaws we might, just might, encounter on our way home. Soon we'll be pulling in pots filled with hair crabs. I think about Freddy's offer to smoke pot. No, thanks. My high will be the money I'll be raking in.

As I lean against the table, I catch a glimpse of a buoy.

"Let's not waste any more time, boys," the skipper says. "Let's start hauling gear." A wide grin stretches across his face.

# Chapter 4

# HAULING GEAR

When we reach the buoys on the first set, the skipper drives the boat next to them while Marv throws a hook out to snag them. Once the line is in the hydraulic block, the skipper comes down from the wheelhouse.

"Haul gear, boys," he yells. Looking over at me, he adds, "Pray for a good catch."

Just because I'm a chaplain's son I should do the praying? I gaze at the deck, too embarrassed to tell him not to count on my prayers.

The skipper stands at the deck controls, using his foot on the floor pedal to control the speed of the line coming in. He maneuvers the boat along the line while Marv unsnaps the pots as they come up and drops them on the table. Meanwhile, the line never stops coming in until the set is finished. I watch closely so I'll know what to do when it's my turn. Again, Marv's gaze pierces me. I shiver.

The line comes in fast. Freddy and I each grab a pot from the table, release the pucker string on the bottom, and shake its contents out. Occasionally we set a pot aside for Erickson to sample. We open the bait jars, dump the old bait overboard, throw the pots to the next man, and sort the crabs.

Our hands fly. We sort crabs by size and sex, throwing the undersized males and all the females overboard. The hair-covered crabs average about three-quarters of a pound. Down a trough go the good ones into the water-filled hold.

A couple hundred pounds of the fragile hair crabs splashing into the tank is music to our ears. We keep catching more and more crabs.

"We're makin' money now!" Freddy yells as we all grin.

But between the sounds of the engines, hydraulics, and line popping in the block, my ears take a beating. As I stop a moment to cover them with my gloved hands, Freddy looks up.

"Noise too much for ya, Horn? Knew ya couldn't take it."

I throw a starfish at him, but he only laughs and ducks. And the crabs keep coming. The hold keeps filling.

The next man in line snaps a fresh bait jar into a pot and stacks the pot near the stern. The last guy stands in the line bin, an open box about five feet wide and fifteen feet long with the stern end open, to coil the line so it will feed back out when we set gear next time.

The hydraulic motor keeps up its thunderous roar. The drone of the diesel engines never lets up night or day. And the wind is picking up again. Guess I never realized how much noise wind makes out on the sea. Cold, wind-driven sea water sloshes over the deck, emptying its stinging spray on my face and eyes.

I help bring in the pots, glad to be regaining some strength. But yesterday's sore muscles only add to more pain today. At least the misery in my stomach is gone.

Freddy and I work side by side for hours. He holds up an extra-large hair crab.

"Hey, Horn. Know the difference between hair crabs and opilios? The hair crabs wear hair nets."

I feel myself turn red as everyone laughs. Anything for a joke at my expense.

Patrick winks at me. "Your joke was better, Jake." He adds, "Seriously, the government allows only fifteen hair crab permits during limited entry fishing. This year's quota is set at two million pounds. That's why we're all racing to get our share."

He points to some of the other boats within the Pribilof area. "Those boats are between ninety and a hundred and twenty feet long. You know already that our boat is the smallest of the fleet. That's why my dad, our skipper, is especially careful. He's as dependable and safe as you can find."

I nod, feeling reassured after Freddy's earlier remarks about williwaws. But Patrick's obsession about his dad concerns me. It's not normal.

In every few pots, we bring in some starfish that have

gone after the bait. Erickson keeps close tabs on such by-catch. Sometimes there are two hundred pounds of starfish in a pot, lowering our money share.

It's the octopuses that the guys hate most. Clearly after the crabs, they slither in and out of the pots from the ocean floor, cleaning out the pots. At times we bring in several empty pots in a row. There's always a cheer on board when we haul in an octopus. That's one less thief of our share.

Night and day become one as we work, despite four hours of sleep out of every twenty-four. There's only one difference between day and night—the light. During the short days—it's November now—we work in the glaring sunlight. As soon as the sun reaches the end of its low arc across the southern sky, it's the row of glaring flood lights overhead that lights our way.

I don't know how the skipper does it. He guides the boat to each line and spends time working on deck, too. His eyes are bloodshot, though, just like the rest of us.

Nearly staggering from fatigue, I stumble when an unusually big wave sweeps across deck. Freddy's hand steadies me faster than I can think.

"Stay clear o' the lines, Horn," he warns. "Or yer crab bait."

My heart pounds in fear. A sudden vision flits across my brain, me being slammed onto the mat by a wrestler's sudden move. Every wrestler's nightmare. Dad's constant reminder comes to mind, too. "God's grace is sufficient, Jacob. His strength is made perfect in your weakness."

Much as I resent the intrusion, I pray, "Lord, please keep me alert."

I calm myself. My stomach rumbles from hunger and I take Marv's lead, rushing to the galley to make a lunchmeat sandwich which I gobble in four bites. This time I dip into the box of granola bars. Any carbs to keep me going.

So much for my meal, whichever one it is. Cheese slices, a PB&J sandwich, jerky, hard salami and mayo slapped on two slices of bread—it's all the same night or day. The meat and potato meals will have to wait for awhile.

During the short trips running between sets, I actually catch a galley nap, cradling my arms as a pillow. Next comes a quick cup of hot, black coffee to keep myself going for another round. We take turns refilling the coffee pot. It's our life juice and we drink gallons of it.

Later, on the way back to St. Paul to unload our crab catch, we finally enjoy a full meal—by Freddy—and a nap. The hold is full to the brim and the price of hair crab is good. Money in the bank, college here I come!

Another round, another trip . . . and another . . . and another. Every five days we dump our full loads at the cannery. Erickson puts in some time keeping the galley clean and doing a little cooking whenever he sees one of us staggering from fatigue. He's a good guy.

Unaware of the time of day or month, I realize it's been many days since I wrote in my journal. Good intentions battle against fatigue every chance I get to write. Poor Joanie. I'll have to try and remember everything that happened so I can fill in later. Right now, it's time for another nap.

One dark morning as we work, Marv asks, "When's Thanksgiving Day, Skipper?" Thanksgiving? I can't believe I forgot about it.

"Already past," the skipper says abruptly, his voice heavy with guilty undertones. My thoughts drift home to Mom and Dad and Joanie helping serve meals at the homeless shelter downtown. It's been a Thanksgiving Day tradition ever since I can remember. I wonder if Joanie was there this year, helping from her seat in the Terminator.

Regret fills my heart. Here I am, too busy to even consider giving thanks. To think about Mom and Dad and Joanie. To remember the good times we've had as a family, meeting those who enjoy the meals we help serve. And too busy to think about our own meal at home that Mom prepared the day after. My eyes fill. I wipe a bait-encrusted glove across them.

Freddy leans next to me as we fill bait jars. "So whad-dya do on Thanksgiving, Horn? Go to church?" His voice reeks with sarcasm.

I mumble an answer. Too tired and depressed to

think, my voice betrays me as I blurt out, "How about you, Freaky Freddy?"

His face darkens. He clenches a bait jar so hard I'm surprised it doesn't break. But he only looks away.

"Thank you, Lord," I breathe. "I almost blew it."

The days and nights creep into early December. Thankfully, the weather holds. It's windy every day, but no big storms have delayed us, only a couple minor snowstorms. The skipper provides a full meal while Patrick guides the *Danny Boy* to St. Paul for the last time. Once we leave for home, the skipper can put her back on auto-pilot and get some sleep. We'll take turns keeping watch.

At St. Paul, Erickson leaves the *Danny Boy*. Our holds are emptied, the catch weighed, and totals tallied for the season. We also unload the crab pots, to be picked up during next year's fishing season. While the skipper takes care of business with the cannery staff, we wait expectantly. He eventually jumps on board, a smile lighting his face.

"Didn't do so well," he tells us. But his fib is obvious. "Actually, you did very well."

He hands each of us a sealed envelope that contains a record of our earnings that we'll collect after we get back to Homer. He heads for the wheelhouse, we free the lines, and we start for home.

## Chapter 5

# THE LONG WAY HOME

Home. I can hardly wait. With trembling hands I open my envelope and peek at the slip inside. Being the greenhorn, I thought I'd receive the smallest cut. I'm surprised and overjoyed to receive eight percent of the net, just as the others did. My share is twice what I expected. I smile all the way to my bunk. Freddy follows me and plops on his bunk.

"I s'pose ya plan to give ten percent to yer church, right, Horn? Seein' yer so religious and all." Again, the sarcasm.

Gritting my teeth, I ignore him and pull out my journal. As I write, he gives up and turns over to face the wall.

*Joanie, it's over! Was too busy to write earlier so I'll have to reconstruct what I did and saw in the past four weeks. My head's in a whirl so this entry will be in bits and pieces.*

*We're on the way home. Home! Never thought I'd miss it but I do. I miss you, too. And Dad and Mom, believe it or not. And I sure miss the solid ground under my feet. And wrestling, which is a breeze compared to crab fishing.*

*The guys are amazing. Even Freaky Freddy surprises me at times. Just when I think he hates me, throwing barbs my way at every turn—and the endless use of "Horn"—he smiles at me. Or winks. He does keep on my back about my faith, though, and that bothers me. It reminds me of all the conversations you and I have had about God. Guess this trip is showing me a side of God I haven't seen since before . . . you know.*

*I don't know what the deal is with Marv. He's a big guy, older, bald, and his mouth is a thin, straight line. It's his eyes that get me, though. He stares holes in me. Soon as I catch him doing it, he looks away. He gives me the creeps.*

*I'm getting used to the constant bouncing of the waves and blowing of the wind. Enough to realize the Bering Sea is awesome beyond belief. The sun shines often, arcing just above the rim of the horizon. Whitecaps dance like diamonds on the waves. Salty spray covers the boat in brilliant shards of ice. Covers us, too, but I'm used to it now. It's too late in the season for whale sightings, but I saw lots of Northern fur seals on St. Paul Island. Plenty of seagulls and cormorants hang around the boat when we dump the old bait out. Sometimes a bird lights on the work table, trying to steal our bait.*

*My hands are always cold, even through my gloves. But I stay fairly warm, thanks to the hard work and to Mom and Dad packing extra long johns and stuff for me.*

I stop writing and think about home. Eight hundred miles to Homer and another two hundred to Anchorage. The time can't go fast enough for me. I'm feeling high about my earnings and about seeing Joanie and the folks again. I can just taste Mom's cooking. I missed out on her famous Thanksgiving dinner, maybe she'll make it again for me. My mouth waters thinking about her apple pies. They're the best.

Next thing I know, Freddy's jostling me about food. Maybe the guy really is psychic.

"Time to eat, Horn."

After a filling meal—spaghetti and meatballs this time, cooked by Marv—I sit at the galley table and relax.

Freddy gets in my face. "Wanna arm wrestle, Horn? I know yer itchin' to get even with me."

I smile. With pleasure I'll beat him. The others move down to make room for us. We finagle a fair way to face each other. Patrick referees. I grab Freddy's right hand in mine, which over the weeks has grown stronger. Why did I bother to bring my dumbbells with me? As if I had time to even use them. Setting and hauling gear kept me in shape.

"Two out of three," Patrick says. "At my count of three."

I grip tightly.

"One, two, three."

I pull hard. Freddy's arm brings mine down in a second. I manage a weak grin. Two more to go. I'll get him next time.

"One, two, three."

I pull harder. Hang on. Grit my teeth. Beads of sweat form on my upper lip and forehead. I practically groan from the pressure. My breath comes in spurts as the seconds go by. The guys shout and pound the table.

"Hang on, Freddy!"

"Get him, Horn!"

"Do him in, Horn!"

Inch by inch, Freddy lowers his arm. I manage to raise mine a little—just before he forces it down with a bang.

Freddy jumps up, raising his arms in victory before slapping me hard on the back. His head is beaded with sweat, too, but he doesn't even breathe hard.

"Guess ya'll hafta come up with another way to get even, Horn. Sorry." Freddy walks away, that freaky grin plastered on his face.

I want to go back to my journal but feel too deflated, even though Patrick and Marv pat me on the back. I lie on my bunk, listening to the droning engines, rocking to the waves and wind, discouraged even knowing I'll soon be home. Which is worse? Losing my camera or losing to Freddy? I doze off to the hum of the engines.

"Wake up, Horn." Freddy nudges me. "Time fer yer watch."

Half asleep, I fill my coffee cup and go up the wheelhouse for my two-hour watch. It's dark. The clock says six. Is it morning or evening? My groggy mind fights to know. Will I ever catch up on my sleep? Knowing everyone else is asleep makes it harder for me to stay awake. I focus on the unseen horizon as the boat rides the waves.

My job is to keep a constant vigil and check the radar so we don't run into another boat. And keep ours on course. And keep an eye on the engine gauges. It's nerve-racking to think the lives of the others are in my hands.

I fight loneliness and fatigue. By the end of my watch, the waves have grown and I add fear to my list of complaints. Once we get on the south side of the Alaska Peninsula, will we face williwaws?

My mind starts playing tricks and my stomach knots up. Once, just before a wrestling match, I got sick. The final match of the season and I was in line for the championship. I had to win but felt like crap. Just wanted to bury my head in my pillow and forget wrestling.

That's how I feel now. I'm not sick but might as well be. If only I could bury my head in my pillow and forget about the rest of the trip home.

But Dad's words come back to me like it was yesterday.

"Buck up, Son, you can do it," he said. "Remember the trials Paul went through on his missionary journeys. He never gave up. Neither did Jesus."

About the time I clear my head and think rationally again, I wake Patrick for the next watch. Giving him time to pour a cup of coffee, I go back up to the wheel. He taps my shoulder. Startled, I jump. I can't be as nervous as he is, though. He's ghostly white and his head and arms jerk. He's no greenhorn, so what's he so nervous about? Isn't he used to the weather after four years of crab fishing with his dad? I head for my bunk.

Jittery as I am, I sleep, not waking until we approach the Aleutians. False Pass will take us out of the Bering Sea into the North Pacific. I go out on deck to get some fresh air, determined not to stand too close to the rail this time.

I wish Joanie could be here. She'd love the feel of the pure wind on her face and the hard, icy spray that assaults the mouth with its salty taste. She could watch the sea change its face every minute. She'd love the endlessly long rollers marching across the miles, white frothy wave tips tumbling down into the deep troughs.

On cloudy days the sea and sky blend into one gray mass. Today is sunny and the long shadow of the *Danny Boy* dances between the rollers. Scenic volcanoes rise in the distance.

A pod of orcas swims by. Totally at ease in the rough sea, they stay within sight, breaching and cavorting, teasing us as we motor ahead of the growing wind. It's easier—less fearful—being out here in their company. If only I had my camera. The only thing I can give Joanie now is the journal.

As we close in to False Pass, I'm amazed at the boiling sea we have to navigate.

Freddy joins me, pointing to the channel markers. "Gotta get over that sand bar first. Then stay in the channel. Not easy, the way it twists and turns."

The tides are right, but still the narrow channel means

a bucking ride through. I feel like retreating to my bunk so I don't have to watch. But I can't help myself, I have to watch. I glance at Patrick, knowing he feels the same way. Will he panic? Will I? As we roll every which way through the pass, I come close to panic.

Once we're through, the seas are calmer and the air feels colder. We motor tight along the mountainous Alaska Peninsula. I relax for awhile, but the thought of williwaws keeps my body wound like a spring. I wish it would be this calm the rest of the way home. But I know better. Any time now, we could be hit by williwaws.

Much later, Freddy joins me and Patrick and Marv in the galley. I can tell from his eyes I'm in for another round of taunts.

"So, Horn, ready for the williwaws?"

"Lay off, Freddy," Marv says.

His comment surprises me.

And I try to surprise Freddy with my own. "You can't scare me anymore, Freddy. You're nothing but hot air. Bet you've never even been in williwaws."

He shrugs, his face serious for once. "We'll see in a day 'er so when we pass them bigger mountains, Horn. We'll see."

My words don't even faze him. Am I such a poor liar? No one else says a word. No one smiles. Do they know something I don't?

Patrick clears his throat and asks, "More coffee, anyone?"

He starts telling us how he's going to spend his

money. Lots of Christmas gifts, he says. Marv joins in with his plans for toys for his two grandsons. It's the most he's said the whole trip and he's smiling, besides. So he does have a life after crab fishing.

"How 'bout you, Horn? Besides college money, that is." Freddy doesn't mention church money this time.

I'm thankful.

I tell the guys what I want to buy for Joanie and my parents, and my dog. But the former, somber mood of the crew bothers me. The feeling of ease I thought I had seeps out of me like a wrung sponge.

Freddy and Marv play a game of poker while Patrick tells me more about the crab fishing area. But I'm not in the mood. After a long while, he gets up.

"Time for my watch," Patrick tells me. "Better get some sleep before your next watch, Jake. It'll be here before you know it."

And it is. After a restless nap, I take over in the wheelhouse. It's a star-studded evening and still windy. Like the last watch, I'm nervous. My thoughts bounce around. About winning a wrestling match last season. About graduation and my friends. About Joanie's accident and how it changed things at home. About Dad scolding me for my sour attitude.

Dad was always spouting Bible verses. It got on my nerves, but somehow the verses stuck with me, ingrained from years of hearing them.

"I can do all things through Christ who strengthens

me," he used to quote—often. Admittedly, he and Mom acted strong while spending hours, night and day, taking care of Joanie. Guess he was trying to tell me God could do the same for me. I'm still not so sure.

And his favorite, "'In everything give thanks, for this is the will of God in Christ Jesus for you.' Keep it in mind, Jacob, when things don't go right."

Guilt settles around me like fog as I ponder a few of the good things about this trip. Things I can be thankful for. It hasn't been all bad. Freddy has been a tad nicer the past few days. The other guys are always respectful of me. Even Marv, with his creepy stare. I earned double the money I expected. My stomach has settled. My muscles have bulked up. Maybe Dad's right.

My watch ends when the skipper comes to takes my place. It's still dark outside and even with the floodlights on, it's hard to maneuver my way back to the bunk. The growing wind keeps me awake.

After an hour or so, the other guys wake up from constant jostling and noisy bangs throughout the boat. We all go up to the wheelhouse to see what's going on.

*Chapter 6*

# WILLIWAW WINDS

"Winds are gusting to 60 knots and the spray is freezing to the boat," the skipper tells us and directs his gaze toward Patrick. "Nothing to worry about. But I'm going to pull into Portage Bay for the rest of the night. Don't want to travel at night in case the winds get worse."

Nothing to worry about? When the skipper looks grim? And Patrick acts like a panic attack in the making? I translate sixty knots into seventy miles an hour. That's hurricane force.

"How do you know the wind speed?" I ask.

"Calculated guess," the skipper tells me. "Our anemometer is broken."

"Sixty knots ain't the worst, Horn," Freddy tells me. "We're used to that. Now williwaws . . . that's a diff'rent story. And this is the place for 'em. Ya might wanna start prayin' the winds don't turn into williwaws."

Freddy isn't trying to scare me this time. He's nervous too, I'm sure. As we huddle in the wheelhouse, things keep banging on deck.

"Double check that everything is secure," the skipper tells Freddy and Marv. "I don't want anything heavy breaking loose."

While they go below to tighten the lines and loose rigging, the skipper motors for the protection of Portage Bay. But he's too cautious to get closer than a half mile out from the bay because of the reefs and shoals.

Patrick and I go down to the galley and fill our coffee mugs while we wait for Freddy and Marv. When they return, they put on a halfway happy face, but I can tell they're worried. Every once in awhile someone tells a joke, but it bombs.

I jump when the anchor drops with a loud rattle.

"Sure hope Dad put out all the anchor cable," Patrick says.

Anchored as we are, the boat sways as much as ever. It's going to be a long night.

Before I decide to go to sleep, the skipper says, "Marv, go down and shut off the main engine. It'll save fuel."

We're doomed if we run out of fuel. I toss and turn on my bunk.

This time it's the skipper who nudges me. "You're on for anchor watch, Jake."

Again? It seems like I just got off.

"Make sure the anchor doesn't drag on the bottom," he tells me as I struggle off my bunk. "We don't want to drift out to sea. It may be rough here, but it's even rougher out there."

At five in the morning it's still dark—halfway through my watch. A crescent moon slides down toward the horizon. Funny how the stars calmly shine down on us while we fight to stay afloat. When I think the winds can't be any stronger, a huge gust from nowhere pushes the boat tight against the anchor cable.

Pow! Like a gunshot the cable snaps. We've lost our anchor.

Instantly the skipper is next to me, grabbing the wheel. "Must have been eighty knots in that williwaw," he mumbles.

Patrick is right behind him, shaking with fear.

Marv restarts the engine. Now what do we do? Maybe it's time to get serious about those prayers I promised God.

The rest of the crew joins us in the wheelhouse.

"Guess all I can do is meander up the coast," he says. "Maybe by dawn the winds will lighten."

It's still dark and by eight o'clock the winds are steady at about sixty knots with many williwaws as strong as the one that broke our inch-thick cable. An eerie, misty light from the floodlights shrouds the boat. Outside the circle of light, it's darker than a closed closet. As we ride the growing waves, I see a glimpse of stars and then, poof! They disappear as we descend into a trough.

"Is it time to call the Coast Guard, Dad?" Patrick's voice quivers.

He stares his dad down until the skipper nods and

then reaches for the radio mike. The nearest base is Kodiak, about a hundred twenty-five miles from here.

Calmly, the skipper relays our position to the Coast Guard station on Kodiak Island. "F/V *Danny Boy,* latitude 57° 30 N, longitude 155° 57, five aboard. No other boats around. We're holding our own, hoping the wind will die down."

He waits until receiving an acknowledgment and then turns to us and smiles. "Just trying to stay on the safe side. We're not giving up yet. But let's pray the weather improves."

I'm scared witless. All of Dad's verses and platitudes and prayers have disappeared in the wind. A chill grabs hold of me, and it's not from the cold.

"Jake, you and Freddy go down and clear the ice from the scuppers," the skipper says. "Don't want the deck filling with water. Secure any loose rigging you find, too."

I follow Freddy down the steps, timing every step with the roll of the *Danny Boy.* On deck, we face tangled rigging whipping about. A coat of ice covers everything. It's so slippery, our neoprene boots don't help us. We cling to the deck rail while we knock the ice out of the scuppers, the openings in the side of the boat at deck level. If they're clogged with ice, water can't run off and the boat will fill with water.

It's exhausting work. But we're not finished. Now we have to secure the mess of rigging on deck. It means more banging ice, more sore muscles, more sweat that's keeping us cold. We finally go back up to the wheelhouse.

As we leave Portage Bay, the winds grow more violent. The skipper has a death hold on the wheel. Patrick stands tight against him, like a child instead of the stocky, grown man he is. The sight makes me want my own dad near.

First the skipper turns the boat into the wind but it makes no headway.

"We're going backwards, Dad," Patrick yells. "Can you turn back?"

"It's our only choice," the skipper says while turning the wheel.

Halfway into the turn, the *Danny Boy* starts to roll hard in a huge wave. I can't see the wave but feel the boat tip to starboard as it plunges into a trough. The skipper can do nothing to help her. The relentless waves come every two seconds. Williwaw gusts add to the rolling.

The skipper's face is pale. He squints, studying the radar, but it's nothing but a blank screen. He must navigate blind, from memory. Now what?

"Better start beating ice, boys," the skipper tells us. "We're getting top-heavy. Seas must be close to sixteen feet and the waves are coming faster. No rest between."

Freddy and Marv hunt in vain for baseball bats to use for beating ice.

"Must've washed over," Freddy shouts. "Can't find any other tools so we gotta use our hands."

The four of us dash below and start beating ice off the rigging. The salty sea spray keeps coming, keeps building. It washes over the deck, coating every surface in its way.

My rubber gloves are no match for the hard ice. In no time, my hands throb from the endless beating and my muscles begin to ache. I want to quit and go lie down.

I look around. "Isn't there anything we can use?"

"The other tools are down in the engine room," Marv says, "but you can't . . ."

I interrupt him and make a dash for the stairway.

Marv jerks me back. "Oh, no you don't. Too dangerous down there right now."

I nod. Disgusted and hurting, I keep my thoughts to myself. No use talking anyway because of the pitiless wind that shrieks through the rigging. I hear a faint grunt, look up, and see Freddy grimacing. He's beating ice for all he's worth, each blow a new ache. I know how he feels. Even though I can't stand the guy, I hate to see anyone else hurting.

Frantic, I look around the cluttered deck. Then I remember my dumbbells. When no one's watching, I slip into the bunkroom and grab them from my duffel. On my way back, I stumble past the galley. Inside, it sounds like bowling balls banging back and forth.

Heading over to Freddy, I yell, "Here, use this," and hand him one of my dumbbells.

He stares at me for an eternity and then nods and starts beating ice. My throat tightens at the look of gratitude and relief in his eyes.

I look upward with my own thoughts of gratitude.

In the misty shadows of floodlight, the radio antennas rock violently back and forth. Will they hold against the williwaws?

Thankfully, the ice breaks off easier and faster using the dumbbells, and my knuckles and wrists quit burning. Even my muscles stop screaming. But I can't keep up with the fast build-up of ice.

Another eternity of beating and I'm about done for. Soaked with chilled sweat, tired, sore, I wonder—how much longer? I remember Dad's favorite verse again. I can do all things through Christ who strengthens me.

"Lord, I need strength!" I shout into the wind. "Save us, please." I bite my lip hard to keep from crying like a baby.

Only the wind answers, formed in another gust. This time the boat rolls over so far, the starboard rail goes under water. Everything goes dark.

"Another williwaw!" Freddy yells. "Let's get off the deck, guys. Let's get to the wheelhouse."

We all scramble up the stairs. It's like walking on a tilted wall. In the crowded wheelhouse the skipper desperately works the wheel.

"The main and auxiliary engines died," he tells Marv. "Get below and start them. We rolled over so far, the fuel lines are sucking air."

Marv grimaces. He grabs a flashlight and hurries below to trip the breakers. We sit nervously, nearly sideways, in the dark. All the lights and electronics are out. The boat slowly rights herself, stuff sloshing all over in the water that keeps coming through the door.

The lights come on as Marv breathlessly returns. "Don't ask me again, Skipper. I know of too many guys who've been trapped in the engine room when their boats rolled over."

Freddy, sitting in a swivel chair bolted to the floor, faces the door. At the next williwaw, I grab his shoulders and hang on for dear life as he tips downward. His legs dangle in the sloshing water pouring in under the door.

"You'd think we were looking into an aquarium, with those starboard windows under water," I say. No one hears me. It doesn't matter.

Again the *Danny Boy* rights itself, this time slower than before.

The skipper grabs the radio transmitter. "Mayday, Mayday," he calls in, repeating the earlier-transmitted information with new latitude and longitude readings. "We're on our side with williwaws . . . waves sixteen feet and very close together," he adds.

I can barely hear him in the wind. While waiting for an answer, the boat rolls ninety degrees again. And again the power goes off.

The skipper slams the microphone on the dashboard. "Radio's gone. Everything's gone."

There goes our only connection to help. Without engine power and communication, we're adrift at the mercy of the sea. It's still halfway dark out. It won't do any good to keep beating ice.

Will it do any good to pray? Without thinking, I start mumbling the Lord's Prayer aloud. Before I finish, the others—all of them—are repeating it with me. How they even hear me over the noise is beyond me.

The skipper's mouth is drawn. Marv runs his hands over his eyes and sniffs. Patrick and Freddy look down until I clear my throat.

"So what do we do now, Skipper?" I ask tentatively.

A look of defeat crosses his face. "It's time to suit up, boys."

Five bright orange survival suits are stored in a box in one corner of the wheelhouse, held tightly behind a bolted chair. The suits are insulated and have enough buoyancy for up to six hours of survival in the cold water. But they're clumsy to put on. During our practice drill on the way out, it took me forever to crawl into mine.

With the boat's violent rocking, it's even harder to get into my suit this time. I manage to pull one leg over my boot, but in desperation I kick off my other boot. Now it's easier. I shrug out of my rain jacket, tug the suit up, zip up the front, and cover my head with the hood. It's tight around my chin; I feel like a stuffed sausage. The other guys are still struggling into theirs except the skipper, who tries to keep order in the room.

"You know your jobs from the drill, boys," he reminds us.

I almost forgot, I'm in charge of the EPIRB—the emergency locator device. I unzip my suit, push the bowling pin-shaped device down into it, and zip it up again. We can't risk losing the EPIRB. It's about twenty inches long and four inches in diameter. Before our trip even started, the skipper had it coded with the name of the boat, destination, his name, and other vital information.

My whole body shakes. The EPIRB slips clear down past my knee.

"Lord, please don't let the EPIRB batteries die," I pray aloud, hoping its flashing light will keep blinking. "Let the signals to the satellite reach someone who can find us."

But then I wonder if the Coast Guard even heard the skipper's Mayday call.

The other guys look somewhat like the orange buoys we send out on our crab pot lines. A hysterical giggle erupts from my shaking gut. Marv's gaze pierces through me. I swallow hard to keep my hysteria down.

The seas are gigantic. If we ever get into our little raft, will we be bobbing in the sea like the buoys at each end of our fishing lines? Will anyone even see our bright suits in these gigantic waves?

Turning my mind to my family and home, I suddenly remember something. "My journal for Joanie!" I yell.

Four sets of eyes turn my way.

Again I swallow hard, this time to keep tears at bay. I've got to control myself. What's a little journal, anyway? But my heart is heavy with regret. First my camera goes, now Joanie's journal.

Dad's words come to mind. "Don't cling to earthly treasures too tightly, Jacob. They'll rot or fade away eventually. Seek God's kingdom and righteousness first. That's what will last to eternity."

Trying to maintain my composure, I look over at Freddy. He's gone! How could he get pulled out to sea while my mind was on other things?

"Freddy!" I yell.

The boat has turned so now the wheelhouse door is over our heads with every roll. Marv bangs the door open and crawls through. Will he find Freddy? When he comes back, will he be able to pull the door open?

*Chapter 7*

# THE RAFT

I hold my breath until Marv and Freddy pound on the door. The skipper manages to push it open and the two men wash down to us in a torrent of water. Freddy shakes himself off, slipping something inside his survival suit.

Now I'm angry. Did he go down to get his stash of pot? Is it that important to him? He zips his suit shut, looks up at the skipper, and yells—acting like nothing happened. The jerk. Just when I was beginning to like and even respect the guy.

"Put yer suit on, Skip," he yells. "She's gonna go down, don'tcha know? Ya can't save her! Don't end up bein' a dead hero."

The skipper's look of despair cuts my heart as he looks at each one of us. We meet his stare, the moment hanging in the frigid air like a fragile bubble. We wait.

Finally he nods and shrugs into his suit. Patrick sits shivering in a chair, his gaze locked on his dad. He's a basket case. He nearly lost his mom and doesn't want to lose his dad.

The skipper tells Freddy and me to free the life raft of ice. I groan with fatigue and fear.

Timing our exit to the wind gusts and waves, we crawl out the topsy-turvy doorway onto the top of the wheelhouse. A williwaw hits the water vertically, like a million angry beavers slapping their tails simultaneously. Water shoots in all directions. The *Danny Boy* bucks like a rodeo bronc. How many more williwaws can she take?

Bolted to the top of the wheelhouse is a small cradle that holds the raft in its canister by heavy straps. The whole mechanism is thickly coated with ice. But before we can free the canister, we must first beat at the ice surrounding the hand rails so we can hang onto them. We don't want to be flung out into the sea.

Freddy and I had the presence of mind to keep the dumbbells with us. We beat the ice until we can hang onto the rails. Then, frantically we beat the ice from the straps that secure the raft canister. We're halfway lying down over the canister, but every williwaw pushes us to an impossible, vertical position. We fight to hold on with one hand while beating ice with the other as we rock back and forth in the wind.

Ice is several inches thick all around the canister. I feel like a roofer trying to secure shingles before the tornado hits.

With every swing of my arm, I repeat a word from Psalm 91 that I learned years ago, that came suddenly to mind.

"I-will-say-of-the-Lord-He-is-my-refuge-and-my-fortress." I take a deep breath. "My-God-in-whom-I-trust."

"Say it again, Horn," Freddy shouts.

Surprised, I beat the words out in a shout this time. Freddy grins at me.

The release mechanism finally works and the straps come loose.

The skipper pokes his head out the doorway. "Launch the raft. Hurry! She's going down soon." He remains in the wheelhouse.

The wind pulls the raft canister out to the end of its hundred-foot cord. Still attached to the cradle, the cord whips around as the canister tosses violently in the sea. The next williwaw gives the canister an extra-hard jerk, releasing the canister's bottle of gas so the raft inflates.

Marv and Patrick join us. We all cling to the hand rails as the *Danny Boy* rocks ninety degrees. Freddy, hanging on with one hand, tries to pull the raft toward us with the other. It's upside down in the waves.

"Pull, Freddy," Marv shouts. "Pull hard. We have to flip it over."

Freddy pulls for all he's worth, but the wind is too strong. The *Danny Boy* turns, bringing the raft—still upside down—tight against the stern. Its line tangles in the rigging, all that rigging we secured earlier that came loose from the violence of the wind and waves. The raft line grows steadily shorter.

We somehow manage to get down to the deck. Hand over hand along the deck rail, we make our way to the stern. Patrick hesitates, again looking back at the wheelhouse.

"Hurry, Dad," he screams. "Hurry!"

How will the raft right itself? We stand there, helpless. In a flash, I hear Dad's voice again. "I can do all things through Christ who strengthens me."

With those words echoing in my head and before anyone else can move, I crawl out on the now-horizontal boom and straddle it. At the next pitch downward, I grab the raft cord and draw it toward me. With an impossible heave of strength, I grasp a strap and flip the raft. Freddy locks onto my leg and helps me crawl backwards to the deck.

"Good work, Jake," the skipper says.

I'm surprised to see him. Patrick clings to his arm, relief evident on his face. As for me, I don't know what I feel more intensely. Elation the skipper is here, or terror at what I just did—or rather what God did. My whole body quivers. But there isn't time to think about it. The raft isn't ready.

"The sides didn't snap up." Freddy speaks the obvious. Not only that, the top is still lying on the raft bottom. Our only means of escape is filling with water.

Before I can think, the skipper has jumped into the raft. By now it's tight against the stern, its ever-tangling line choking it.

"Come on, boys, hurry," the skipper shouts. "Help me with the roof."

The skipper looks grim. I know what he's thinking. The captain always goes off the ship last, but for the sake of his crew, he had to go first.

We don't have much time. But how can we manage to stay in that little thing, open to the elements as it is? We can't, I'm sure of it. A taste of metal fills my mouth. I try to swallow, but fear makes me gag.

By the time the rest of us are ready to jump, the skipper has managed to get the sides up. One by one, we crawl along the swinging boom out to the raft.

Patrick jumps, clearly desperate to be close to his dad.

"You next, Marv," the skipper says. "Hurry, I need your weight."

Immediately following Marv's jump, Freddy gives me a thumbs up. "Yer next, Horn. Hurry. Don't leave me here alone."

This time crawling along the boom, I'm terrified. I cling to the slippery ice. Every time the boom swings, my muscles tighten. My heart pounds like a bass drum. The tiny raft bounces on huge, icy waves that churn like a gigantic washing machine.

I look back on the *Danny Boy*. So big and sturdy—so close to sinking. Swallowing hard against a mouthful of cotton dryness, I inch my body along the boom. The guys in the raft beckon me frantically.

I mumble Dad's verse. I can do all things through

Christ who strengthens me. I can do all things through
Christ who strengthens me. I can do all things. . . .

My heartbeat slows. Timing the waves, I jump.
Actually, it's not as far down as I thought. But just as I
make the leap, a williwaw jerks the raft away. I hit water.
Down I go. Down . . . down . . . down. Panic-stricken, I
flail my legs and arms until my buoyant suit pushes me
upward. Right next to the raft.

I reach for one of the handholds on the outside of the
raft. If not for them, I'd never make it inside because I
feel like I've just sprinted two miles. Even then, it takes
Marv to help haul me in. I cough, sputter, and manage
to sit up on the raft bottom in icy water.

Freddy jumps and crawls in. We're finally all together.

"Thank you, Lord," I shout, "for survival suits and
friends." At that moment I realize God answered my
prayers. Grateful beyond belief, my throat thickens. My
eyes fill. Pretending to wipe them free of salty sea, I bite
down to stop my lips from quivering.

A loud bang pulls me back from emotional fallout.
It's the boom. It hits against the raft, throwing the skipper out. He arcs through the air like a rag doll.

"No!" Patrick leaps toward the opening.

Marv catches him by the arm and jerks him back in.
I gasp as the skipper disappears into a trough and then
pops up a few yards out. Swimming hard, he reaches us.
Marv hauls him in.

The skipper is no sooner settled—if I can call it

that—and the boom knocks Freddy out this time. When he reaches us, he's gasping for air, eyes closed, a big knot already forming on his forehead.

The skipper helps him into the raft and checks for further injuries. "You'll be fine," he tells Freddy. "The icy water will keep the swelling down. Feel okay?"

Freddy nods.

"Good. Okay, boys, we have to get this top up. On the count of three, start lifting."

We space ourselves around the raft and kneel, trying to slide under the top that's lying on the bottom under water. It's hard to maneuver with one leg stiff and straight from the EPIRB being along my knee.

"Okay. One . . . two . . . three," the skipper says.

We all reach down and lift the top. It weighs a ton under all the water. Grunts and groans grow louder as we lift it. One last effort brings it out of the water so we can push it up. It snaps into place and stays put. Thank God.

There's enough room for us all and the raft holds us comfortably except when williwaws shove us into each other. Like two stacked donuts, the raft is about eight feet across and three feet deep. Water covers the bottom donut and partway up the top one. A person could drown in here.

As it tosses us around, I feel like a Lilliputian doll. I cling to the lines that are strung along the edge of the top donut.

The skipper is digging inside a pocket attached to the

side of the raft. "Where's the knife, boys? We've got to get free of the boat." The skipper searches frantically.

The raft is full of debris. Ties, flares, tools, and other junk float haphazardly in the water. But no knife.

Freddy, shivering, unzips his suit, finds a knife in his pants pocket, and starts cutting lines. As he saws through the tangled lines, another williwaw hits. The *Danny Boy* pushes the raft under water. Desperately, we cling to our handholds.

Freddy's knife flips out of his hand, landing at Patrick's feet. Marv reaches down, his head submerging in the splashing water. When he raises himself up, he opens his hand to reveal a bunch of junk—including the knife. I breathe another prayer of thanks.

Freddy cuts away at the lines. He looks on the verge of collapse. I grab his wrist to add strength to his hand as he keeps sawing. Every cut becomes a prayer in my head, on my lips. The skipper hangs onto Freddy to keep him in the raft.

Too much is happening too fast. The sun is shining. This isn't even a "storm." But the wind and waves are more furious than in many storms. I'm in the worst possible, heart-pounding, reality TV drama. My brain freezes up. In a haze, I feel the last line grow thinner. I blink hard to clear my head just as we cut through it.

As though fired from a cannon, our released raft blows out to sea. I take a death grip onto the handholds, gulping at the suddenness of our freedom. All of us are jerked backward and end up flailing in the water on the floor.

Will the steep seas roll our raft over? How long can we hang onto our handholds? Who'll be the winner of this wrestling match? Five puny people huddled in a tiny raft that loses its way between gigantic waves? Or the williwaws?

Will we even see our families at Christmas? Will I see Joanie again? The loss of my camera and journal seem insignificant compared to the potential loss of our lives. But I still want to be able to share all the details of this trip with Joanie. I promised. So I struggle to blaze each moment into my memory. For her sake. She's counting on me.

Click. I take a mind picture of the next williwaw wave. Click, another one, of us crab fishing. Click, us huddled in the raft looking like drowned pups. Click, one more. The *Danny Boy* wallowing in the sea.

Through the raft opening, I stretch to look at the *Danny Boy*. She's bobbing in the water a quarter mile away. Then . . .

"Look," I yell.

We all watch silently as the *Danny Boy's* bow sinks deeper into the sea. The next wave crests and she's gone. The skipper turns his head, his lips drawn in a tight line. He must feel like he lost his best friend.

I close my eyes against the horror of nearly going down with her and I thank God for another miracle.

Relief washes through me.

But there's no time to relax. The raft rides a mountainous wave only to plunge into a runaway roller coaster. One wave after another. Will we ever get time to rest? How long can we hold on until our muscles give out? Mine feel as tight as rubber bands. My stiff leg aches. The world's biggest roller coaster would be like falling into a pile of snow compared to this heart-stopping ride we're on.

I grab a verse Dad repeated a lot. "Be anxious for nothing, but in everything by prayer and supplication, with thanksgiving, let your requests be made known to God; and the peace of God, which surpasses all understanding, will guard your hearts and minds through Christ Jesus." Lord, help me not to be anxious in this life-death situation. Help me be thankful right now. Give me Your peace that passes all understanding by helping me keep my mind on You more than on the williwaws.

## Chapter 8

# THE WAIT

Freddy and the skipper both shiver. Freddy isn't as skinny as the skipper, but when he opened his suit, water must have seeped in and soaked him to the bone. His eyes remain closed.

"Jake, check the EPIRB," the skipper yells between his chattering teeth. "Pull it out of your suit and hang onto it."

I unzip my suit partway as we travel up a wave, and pull on the antenna to bring the EPIRB out. Yes! The flashing light is still on. Cradling the EPIRB in one arm, I ask God to help me not lose it. And I ask Him to send its signal straight to the Coast Guard. Better yet, to a helicopter on its way to rescue us.

It's not easy hanging on with one hand and clutching the slippery EPIRB with my other arm. But at least I'm not shivering like Freddy and the skipper. My legs and feet are cold from the sloshing water, but I can take it. How long can they take their shivering?

We sit quietly, scattered around the raft for balance. Sometimes Marv's eyes are closed and I wonder what he's thinking. Other times his gaze drills holes in me. Patrick sits huddled next to his dad as if to keep him from shivering. Freddy's features are tight as a wire spring.

I close my own eyes, picturing Mom at home. It must be around ten in the morning by now. Mom is getting ready to drive Joanie to therapy. Dad has left for work, probably going over the chapel message he'll give later this morning. Do any of them have a clue about our situation? Has anyone called them about us?

Someone slides next to me. I look up, startled to see the skipper.

"Jake, pray for us, will you?"

"You mean out loud?" The inside of my mouth turns to straw.

The skipper nods. Everyone leans forward, waiting to hear my voice.

The skipper doesn't know that I've never prayed aloud in a group. Not even for my family. Dad tried to encourage me endless times, but I never would. Not that I didn't pray. But . . . here? I know these guys. What'll they think if I mess up?

Thoughts about the trip skip across my brain like foam-tipped waves. Thoughts like how I managed to stay awake with little sleep for almost four weeks. How I went hours with nothing to eat. How I put up with sweaty clothes spattered with smelly fish bait. How I heaved boxes and pots and lines endlessly. How I dumped crabs, sorted crabs, threw away undersized crabs till I never wanted to see another crab.

I learned how to run the boat . . . how to read the tides . . . how to walk on deck in the wind without falling. I even learned to take Freddy's mouthy comments without putting him in a scissors lock.

Everything I did and learned came from working with these guys as a "well-oiled machine," as the skipper said earlier. There's nothing I could have done alone. Different as we are in looks and personality, we depended on each other.

We still depend on each other. We're not out of the water yet. And now, at this moment, the guys are depending on me to lead them in a prayer. How can I refuse?

I remember another verse Dad used to quote every time I complained. "Rejoice in the Lord always. And again I say, rejoice." It always sounded weird but I can try it.

Nodding my head, I begin.

"We, um, thank You, God, for getting us this far with Your miracles and for the skipper's good leadership . . . and, um, for friends . . . and for keeping us from getting hurt. Even the bump on Freddy's head is gone. And for helping us get into the raft . . . and for keeping us together . . . and for getting us out of all the tight spots. God, we pray the EPIRB won't fail. Please let the Coast Guard hear its signal so they can find us. Please don't let the EPIRB fail. Please keep the rescue team safe. Please rescue us from this, um, awful situation. And keep the raft from rolling over. We want to see our families again.

Save, us, God. And, um, keep the skipper and Freddy from getting too cold. In Jesus' Name I pray. Amen."

"Amen," the guys add in husky voices before they lean back.

Freddy winks at me. The skipper closes his eyes and smiles. Patrick's pinched look is gone. The scowl on Marv's face disappears but he keeps staring at me. I smile at him, no longer fearful of his sinister looks.

I actually feel some peace. It reminds me of the song my mom used to sing while she cooked, a song about peace like a river, about sorrows rolling away like sea billows, and about God saying it is well with my soul. The words make sense to me now.

But it's not over yet. I take a deep, shaky breath. Still in the praying mood, I make a silent deal with God. He's done well so far. I can't believe I'm saying that. Anyway, if He gets us back home, I promise I'll trust Him from now on and won't complain when things go wrong—like when I lose a wrestling match. Or when I lose patience with Dad. And I promise to spend more time with Joanie. I won't let God down. Not again.

The skipper shouts for our attention. "We need to plan who'll be rescued first, when the helicopter crew comes for us. Freddy, you go first since you're shivering and have an injury. Jake, you go next, then Marv and Patrick. I'll go last."

"No way, Dad! I won't leave you." Patrick looks ready to cry.

The skipper sighs. "You go when I say, Patrick."
The skipper's voice is uncharacteristically firm. But
it softens when he turns to the rest of us. "We'll get
out of this, guys. Don't worry." His words ring with
confidence.

Freddy and I take turns watching for a chopper. He
also checks his waterproof watch while we climb a wave.

"It's been ninety minutes, guys. Think they'll be here
soon?"

The words are hardly out of his mouth when a chopper flies by. When we reach the top of another wave, I
look out and see it. A big, beautiful helicopter way up
high. I practically jump up and down.

Patrick fires a flare but the wind takes it away. The
chopper didn't see us. My heart drops into a trough of
hopelessness. Upturned mouths flatten. Mine included.

"Lord, You didn't mean this to happen, did You? Aren't
you going to let them see us? You can't do this to us!"

The guys stare at me. Did I say that out loud? Right
after my pretty prayer? How dumb. My face heats up so
I look away.

I mumble more whiney prayers. Israelite wilder-
ness prayers, Dad calls them, referring to God's people
complaining in the desert even though God had rescued
them from the Egyptians by parting the Red Sea and
performing other miracles.

Just as I try to reckon God's rescues with our own
situation, the noise from the chopper flying high over-

head fills the air again. Maybe they did get the EPIRB signal. My prayers change. Pleading prayers this time.

The next chopper I hear sounds much lower. When I stick my head out the opening, stinging ice pelts my face. Waiting for the right moment, I open my eyes. The small chopper hovers almost above us. I grin, give a thumbs-up. We cheer.

We take turns peering out into the icy waves. The rotor blades keep up a chop-chopping noise that drifts in the wind, loud then muffled, over and over.

It's Freddy's turn to look. "It's a swimmer," he shouts. "Yes!" He raises his arm and closes his fist in a victory sign.

I grab a peek. In seconds a bright orange apparition reaches our raft. He's wearing a mask with a snorkel, and fins on his feet.

"Good morning, boys," he says. "I'm Marty. Is everyone here?"

We jabber like harbor seals, letting him know we're all here and okay. He quickly looks us over.

"You first," he tells the skipper. "How long you been shivering?"

"But I thought . . . I mean . . . Freddy should . . ."

Marty repeats himself. "You first, Captain."

The skipper's shoulders slump. I know he's worried about Patrick. As he moves to the opening and steps out, Patrick leaps up.

"No! No, Dad, you can't leave me."

It takes Freddy and me both to hold him back. I try for a hammerlock to his arm but he jerks away. With Freddy's help, I put Patrick in a headlock and yank him back to the farthest side of the raft. We practically have to sit on him while his dad swims off with Marty.

It's obvious, none of us wants to split up. We've been like family. It's like I should have felt when I left Joanie, if I hadn't been such a jerk.

But it's time to split up. Not for long, I pray.

*Chapter 9*

# THE RESCUE

Marty guides the skipper through the waves to the metal basket bouncing on the water. I wish it were closer. Marty helps the skipper in and up he goes, the basket swinging in the wind. Before the skipper even reaches the chopper during his ascent, Marty's back at the raft.

"You're next," he tells Freddy. "How long you been shivering?"

"I ain't shiverin'."

Marv laughs in his face. "Yeah, right. You're soaked through and through. To quote you, 'Don't be a dead hero.' Remember?"

No one says a word. Marty helps Freddy into the icy water. How fast can the swimmer get us all up safely? This time around, the raft has drifted and is farther away. It takes Marty forever to reach us again.

"You're next," he tells Marv.

Marv is clearly reluctant. He stares at me until Marty tells him to hurry.

Patrick can't sit still. I pray he doesn't panic again.

Marv goes up but the swimmer doesn't come back. When the basket lowers, he climbs in and is lifted up into the chopper. Pointing, Patrick becomes incoherent and I nearly panic. Are they out of fuel? It's over a hundred miles to Kodiak. Will we survive before they refuel and return? It's daylight now, but they'll never get there and back before dark. We'll die. With three guys gone, the raft is lighter. It bobs violently, the water sloshing all over us.

The chopper doesn't leave, only hovers above us for a while and then repositions itself closer to us. Finally Marty is lowered and swims back.

"Sorry, guys. Had to take a little rest. Your raft kept blowing farther and farther away. It took all I had to swim back and forth. We're on target now. How about you next?" He points to me.

I shake my head hard. "No, Patrick will go berserk. You have to take him."

The swimmer nods. "Come on then," he says, and guides Patrick out of the raft.

I've never felt so alone. I sing. I talk to myself. I conjure images of Mom's Christmas dinner and a tree surrounded with gifts and Joanie and . . . . Mostly, I pray.

Next thing I know, Marty's back.

"Last man out," he says with a hearty laugh.

He pulls me from the raft, hanging on to me with a death grip, and manages to take a knife from his sealed, outer pocket. I'm astonished as he slices a long gash through the top and bottom layers of the raft.

He grins. "That's so no one will find an empty raft and wonder if anyone drowned."

The EPIRB I dropped in the raft long ago will go down with it.

I'm exhausted. Even with Marty's help, even with the basket closer than before, it takes forever to swim to it. Waves push us and cover us and batter us. They dunk us repeatedly. I think of the clown at the County Fair who's dunked by the ball hitting the bulls-eye. I'm the clown but not by choice.

We finally reach the basket. At least the cable looks thicker from this angle than it did from the perspective of the raft. The basket reminds me of a grocery cart without wheels. There's room for only one person with his knees scrunched up tight.

I climb in with Marty's help. Tucking my legs against my chest, I grip the edges as a huge wave dunks me and the basket. I come up sputtering and coughing. Then . . . up, up I go.

What a ride! Once I clear my eyes of sea water, I look down. My heart leaps to my throat. As far as I can see, huge, white cresting rollers chase each other across the sea. They seem to cover the whole world. The basket swings in wide arcs as we go up.

Oddly enough, I become acutely aware of the sea's beauty and God's awesome creation. My heart swells thinking about His majesty.

Once inside the chopper, I collapse on the floor next to the other guys while we wait for Marty to board.

Wrapped in blankets, the guys give me a high-five like I'm a long-lost friend. Even Freddy smiles through his blue-tinged mouth. His eyelids droop.

The chopper dips into a turn toward Kodiak. While the two pilots speak to each other through their earphones, their mouths tense, the basket crane operator peers intently through the side door. What's wrong?

Marty sits behind us, listening to the pilots through his earphones. The skipper yells something to him. He slips the phones off and explains what's going on. I can barely hear him. I sit up to check out the dashboard instruments. Red lights are flashing everywhere on the panel. What does that mean? It can't be good.

"Never been in such bad conditions before, the pilot told me," Marty says. "We're out of de-icer so they can't see out the windows even at a hundred fifty feet up."

"Think we'll make it home?" the skipper asks.

"We have a tail wind so that should help save fuel. But the engine is racing, causing us to use fuel too fast. Got to get out of this spray so the ice will melt."

The chopper bucks and bounces as it struggles to rise above the icy spray from the waves. In my groggy haze, I sense their feelings of urgency.

Marv scoots close to me. "Been watching you, Horn," he says next to my ear.

I smile. "As if I didn't know."

He actually smiles in return. "You've changed. You're a man now."

I ponder his words. If I am, it's because the guys were there for me in spite of their teasing—and so was God.

"When we get back, will you help me find something?" Marv asks.

I nod.

"I want a Bible so I can look up those verses you said."

I'm stunned. "Uh, sure, Marv. I'll need a new one, too, since mine is at the bottom of the ocean. We can go shopping together . . . if we get home." I don't tell him that my Bible lay tucked at the bottom of my duffel all those weeks, unopened and unread.

The chopper keeps bucking and sputtering. As I fight sleep, I can't help but wonder if the williwaws will win this wrestling match yet. At the moment I'm too tired to care and fall asleep. A couple hours or more pass when the chopper motor takes on a different sound. Raising myself on my elbows, I peer through the now-clear window.

Land! At long last the chopper touches ground.

Marv, Patrick, the skipper, and I scramble out of the chopper. It's past lunchtime and the sun shines brightly. The air is calm, the calmest since I left Homer's Kachemak Bay six weeks ago. I revel in the quietness.

Freddy's in no shape to move. Asleep, or maybe unconscious, he's carried to a gurney by two medics. They remove his survival suit and lift him onto the gurney.

"Take it easy, Freddy." I touch his arm as I walk beside the gurney. My throat clogs up. I wish he didn't have to go.

"Horn," he practically whispers. He fumbles in his jacket pocket. "Yours," he says, handing me a soggy item. He winks at me, closes his eyes, and drops his limp arm onto his chest.

The men whisk him away to an ambulance standing by.

I look down at my hand. My journal. I'm stunned. The scene in the wheelhouse rushes back to me. Freddy's disappearance. While I worried about him, felt angry with him, he risked his life to retrieve my journal.

I clutch the soggy book to my chest and swipe my eyes with a wet sleeve.

"Come on, Jake." The skipper places his hand on my shoulder. "It's warmer inside."

Tripping over my feet, I'm almost tipsy from exhaustion and sea legs. And gratefulness.

Once inside the chopper hanger, we shrug out of our suits. An officer escorts us into a small office where several other Coast Guard men greet us. After introductions, he wastes no time in getting down to business.

"Sorry for the delay. I know you're eager to get home, but we have to go through this debriefing." He hands the skipper a small cup. "We have to collect a urine sample from you. It's standard procedure. You know how it is—just to make sure the boat didn't go down because you were on drugs."

We sit around a table while the skipper leaves and then returns to answer questions. His monotone and deep sighs suggest how devastated he feels about losing the boat.

"Right up to the last, even when she lay on her side a couple of times, I didn't want to accept defeat," he tells the Coast Guard crew.

The room buzzes with talk, our heroic chopper crew the center of conversation. I keep one ear open to their comments while the skipper goes through the debriefing.

"I've never seen anything like it in thirteen years of flying," the pilot tells his co-workers who crowd around him. "Those were the worst weather conditions I've ever experienced. Our chopper picked up sea spray at four hundred feet."

"Yeah, I expected to find either bleeding men or corpses in the raft," Marty says. "When I reached them, I couldn't believe they were all okay. A little panic from one, some hypothermia in another, but all willing to help in their own rescue. It was a miracle."

"They did everything right," the pilot adds. "They had the raft ready, their suits on, and without their EPIRB beacon we wouldn't have found them. They saved themselves."

God helped a lot, too, I'm thinking. If not for Him, we truly would be corpses. I agree with Marty. It was a miracle.

When the skipper is released he places a call to his business partner, who owns a share in the *Danny Boy*, to tell him the bad news about the boat. He also explains that we need immediate accommodations. The rest of us take turns calling our families.

My voice isn't the only husky one as I talk to my mom and dad. Mom's sobs start my eyes watering. Sniffing hard, I ask, "So will you make me a Thanksgiving meal?"

She chuckles, agreeing, then puts Joanie on the line.

"I have a big surprise for you!" Joanie starts out. "So does Dad. When will you be home? I can hardly wait."

We talk and laugh some until a uniformed officer steps into the room.

"I'll give you a ride downtown so you can get some dry clothes," he tells the skipper.

"Gotta go, Joanie. See you tomorrow. Check the airlines for our arrival."

"The store closes in fifteen minutes," the officer says, hurrying us toward his vehicle. "We're twelve miles from town."

After scrambling to leave amid handshakes and back pats, we climb in the vehicle, clutching the blankets wrapped around our wet bodies. After feeling so lethargic from the warmth of the office, I shiver in the cold and cover my wet head with the blanket. My bootless feet freeze through their soggy socks.

The warm, twelve-mile ride to town lulls me to sleep. With a jolt I wake up. We've arrived at the store, but the door is locked. The skipper pounds on the glass until a short, round, bald man opens up. Our dismal condition makes his eyes bug out. I follow the others as the skipper explains our situation to him.

"The store's all yours, boys," he says, his voice thick

with emotion. "Pick whatever you need. I'll stay open all night for you if I have to."

But we're too tired and miserable to spend much time shopping, so we hurry to select new underwear, jeans, shirts, socks, boots, hats, gloves, and jackets. The officer graciously waits in his vehicle for us to finish before dropping us off at the local hotel.

Once inside our hotel room and showered at long last, we're too keyed up to sleep. We talk and watch TV until exhaustion catches up with us. My last thoughts before sleep are, tomorrow I'll be home.

We awake early, dress in our new clothes, and catch a taxi ride to the airport where Freddy meets us after an early release from the hospital.

The airplane ride to Homer is smooth, dry, and warm. My thoughts wander back to the day I boarded the *Danny Boy* and everything that happened between then and now. I've been gone six weeks. How much has changed since then? The world has moved on, but I haven't. Thinking about all the adjustments I'll have to make causes my stomach to bounce in spite of the smooth ride. And what about Joanie—will she be worse, or better? Who will be there to meet me? What's the big surprise my family has waiting for me?

## Chapter 10

# HOMECOMING

As I step into the small Homer terminal, there's Mom and Dad with Joanie between them. Are my eyes deceiving me? Is that Joanie pushing a walker? Where's the Terminator?

I run to greet them, my face stretching tight into a grin. Both Mom and Dad try to hug me at the same time, Mom sobbing the whole time. Joanie stands still and watches, tears streaming down her cheeks.

"Hey, come meet my friends, Joanie." I clear the lump in my throat and drape my arm around her shoulder as we head over to the crew. I introduce her to Patrick, Freddy, Marv, and the skipper. Their smiles are broad as they politely shake hands with Joanie. Mom and Dad have already met the skipper. His wife is there, too, along with Freddy's mom and two sisters.

For a few seconds, it's quiet. Uncomfortable. Until Freddy clears his throat.

"Hey, Horn. Let's get together next Saturday. Okay?" His gaze travels from me to the others.

"Sounds good to me," the skipper says. "Maybe your checks will be in by then."

The others agree to meet.

"How 'bout the Salty Dawg Saloon about noon?" Freddy asks and then looks sheepish. "Naw, better make it the café downtown."

I look at Dad. "Can I borrow your car and come down?"

He and Mom exchange looks, their eyes sparkling. Joanie giggles. What's that all about?

"Sure, Son. That'll be fine," Dad says. "I'm sure you guys have lots to talk about."

"You've lost weight, Jake," Joanie says. "Guess your friends can't call you 'Beef' anymore. 'Lean Beef' is more like it."

Oh, brother. I roll my eyes. Freddy turns his head to stifle a laugh.

"See ya later, Horn," he says and leaves, along with the skipper and Patrick and their families.

As Dad drives us and Marv downtown, I explain our reason to shop. At the bookstore Dad helps Marv choose a Bible that will help him understand the verses. I choose one like the one I lost at sea.

"I'll be praying for you, Marv," I tell him as we pull up next to his pickup back at the harbor. "Here's my number. Call whenever you have questions."

Marv nods, grips my shoulder, and ducks out of our car.

On our long drive to Anchorage, we're all quiet at first, everyone waiting for me to talk, I guess. As usual, Joanie breaks the ice with a silly question.

"So how did you lose so much weight?" she asks.

"Crabbing is hard work, Sis. Takes a lot out of a person . . . and the meals aren't that great. Actually, the meals we had time to cook were okay. Just not enough of them."

My answer unleashes a barrage of questions they fire at me so fast I can't keep up. I don't mention the camera. But then . . .

"Did you take lots of pictures?" Joanie asks.

As I stammer out the words I hate to say, Dad pats my knee.

"It's okay, Jacob. Don't worry."

It's dark when we get home and Dad pulls up to the garage door. I'm still tired from the whole ordeal so I forget to ask why he doesn't park in the garage. Before going to bed, I watch Joanie maneuver around the house with her walker.

"I call this Terminator Two," she says, beaming. "Doc says another month of therapy, and I'll graduate to crutches. And by summer maybe a cane."

"Wow, Joanie. I'm glad. Do they think you'll walk normally again?" I hold my breath, waiting for her answer.

"Maybe. Just maybe. No promises, Doc said. I'm thankful to be this far." She looks into my eyes. "Aren't you, Jake? Can you see the miracle in it?"

"Yeah, I can." This time I have to agree with her. "It really is a miracle."

The next morning, Dad says, "Let's go for a ride, Jacob."

I'm surprised because he usually doesn't ask me to go out with him. But now he leads me out to the double garage and invites me to take the wheel of a red Maverick sitting where his car is usually parked. No wonder he left the car out all night.

He hands me the keys. "Consider this an early seventeenth birthday gift."

My legs turn to rubber. My eyes mist for a moment and then I catch the excitement of having my own car. "How cool is this, Dad? Thanks."

"Your skipper told me you did a fine job, Son." His voice is gentle. "And your faith and courage inspired the crew to keep going."

"But, Dad. It was the crew that inspired *me* to keep going. I don't deserve any of the credit. They were the best."

"Don't sell yourself short, Jacob. I have a letter from the skipper to prove my words. Now let's give this baby a whirl. It's yours, Son. You earned it."

I climb in, back up, and take my dad for a drive. Around the whole city of Anchorage. I'm in heaven.

Later, while I head down the street toward home, Dad turns to me. "So did you wrestle with God for the blessing, Jacob?"

His question takes me by surprise because even while tooling around town, my thoughts were heavy on Freddy and the other guys. Can't seem to shake them from my mind . . . like we're still working together trying to survive.

"Yeah, I did, Dad." I tell him about my early struggles with my faith and how that all changed during the storm. I share a lot more, too. Man stuff about the guys I worked with.

Our ride ends too quickly. Again I thank Dad for the car.

"I'm proud of you, Son." He gives me a bear hug. "You've grown up."

The next Saturday I drive Mom to Homer so she can visit her sister while I hang out with the guys at the café.

"This is a good excuse for you to come down with me again, Jake," Mom says as she exits the car. "Good for both of us. Maybe I'll see my sister more often." She winks at me.

In the café, I feel out of place at first as the guys talk about the fishing business, our rescue, and about other accidents at sea.

The skipper taps his glass for attention. "Guys, I heard from my insurance company and it's a go for all of you being reimbursed for your losses. Clothes, electronics, anything that went down with the *Danny Boy*. They'll be sending you forms to fill out and send back. Shouldn't be long before you receive your checks."

He picks up a small briefcase propped against his chair. Grinning, he opens it and with a flourish, hands us each a check for the fishing trip. "A little bonus, too, boys. Compliments of my partner and me."

I find a thousand dollars tacked on to what I expected.

"You deserve it. All of you."

We hem and haw our thanks and everything turns quiet until Freddy rescues us.

"So what's this about Beef, Horn? Can I call ya Lean Beef since yer not a horn no more?"

No longer angered at his ribbing, I laugh. "Sure, Freddy. I'm now the Lean Beef of the crew—even if you did win at arm wrestling."

"So yer sayin' yer gonna fish again next year?"

I shake my head. "Not in the winter. But maybe I'll follow Patrick's advice and fish in the Pribilofs during the summer. I'll be off school then."

We keep jabbering. I like these guys. After a couple hours it's time to pick up Mom. As we say our goodbyes, the skipper pulls me aside.

"Patrick isn't going to fish with me anymore. Thought you'd like to know. He's getting some counseling for awhile and plans to enroll at the university. Maybe you'll see him there."

I'm glad. Patrick's a good guy. A little panicky, that's all.

"And Jake," the skipper continues, "if you change your mind, there's always room on my boat for you.

That is, when I get another boat." He grins as he shakes my hand.

"Hey, Horn!" Freddy says. "If ya can't take the heat of them williwaws," he jabs me hard in the arm, "ya can always spend the summer at fish camp. I know just the camp fer ya. Off Kodiak."

Fish camp? I'll have to check that out. It might be easier on my stomach. And no williwaws.

Freddy shakes my hand, looks me in the eye, and says, "Let's get together again soon, Beef. You can help me tease my sisters. And eat some o' Mom's good home cookin' . . . and try to win the next arm wrestlin' round." He winks.

Freddy and me friends? Wow.

"I'd like that, Freddy."

I really would.

# THE REAL STORY

*WILLIWAW WINDS* is based on a true story of how my son and four others were rescued from sea much like the characters in this book. While I've changed the names and personalities of the real men, much of my story really happened.

The skipper started out in late October of 1996 on his boat when crab fishing for hair crabs was considered "limited entry" fishing. That means the government allowed a certain number of pounds of hair crabs to be caught within a short time by a small, prescribed number of boats. Since then, the law has changed. It's easier for fishermen and women today because they own percentages of the quota and have a much longer season to work at it. That means when bad weather comes, they can sit it out instead of having to hurry for their catch before the short time is up.

The real crew of five worked day and night without time for sleep. One week they figure they slept an hour each, plus a few cat naps. The work was as hard as the story tells. Unlike my story, the real crew had a bad catch that year and went home with little money.

Facts about the sinking of the boat are true. Like Marv in the story, my son was the engineer. And like Marv, he refused to go down to the engine room the third time for fear of losing his life there. Unlike in the story, no one became hypothermic.

Today my son owns a thirty-four-foot fishing boat which he uses each summer to fish halibut and cod around the Homer and Kenai Peninsula area, with the help of his son during summer college break. In the winter my son flies to his trap line west of Fairbanks where he catches marten, mink, beaver, wolverines, and an occasional lynx.

The heroic helicopter crew from the Kodiak Coast Guard station include pilots Jeff McCullars and F. Carl Riedlin, swimmer Mike Mille, and basket crane operator Mark Clark. Bill Vieth was Commander of the station back then. Each crew member was awarded the Distinguished Flying Cross, the highest award for airmen, for their heroic efforts in saving the fishing crew.

The Kodiak Coast Guard crews continue to rescue men and women from harm in the Bering Sea and northern Pacific—with God's help.

## About the Author

**Sally Bair** has written numerous children's books and is currently writing the second in the "Ways of Williwaw" series, entitled *Trouble at Fish Camp*. She writes a weekly devotional column, "Eternal Perspectives," for local newspapers. A former journalist, Sally also has written ad copy, public relations articles, and freelance stories and articles. She has won several awards for her stories.

Sally enjoys inspiring others through her speaking engagements and mentoring young girls in creative writing. She loves reading, writing, gardening, and communing with nature.

The mother of three children, Sally enjoys her ten grandchildren and one great-grandchild when she can. She makes her home in Wisconsin near the south shore of Lake Superior.

# Hey kids, I'd like to hear from you!

After reading *WILLIWAW WINDS*, you know what a williwaw is. Let's think of a williwaw as a storm of life—such as your parents going through a divorce, a death or illness in the family, or a move away from your friends and loved ones.

What kind of williwaw have you had in your life?

How did you handle it?

With someone else's help?

With God's help?

Alone?

Please share your thoughts and stories with me and my readers.

Go to www.cedarhavenbooks.com

or www.sallybair.com

Or write me at: Sally Bair
c/o Cedar Haven Books
P.O. Box 186
Washburn WI 54891

**Look for my sequel:** *Trouble at Fish Camp*

# Experience the Adventure!

*WILLIWAW WINDS* is an inspirational adventure story of Jake, a rebellious teenager who goes out to the Bering Sea with a crab fishing crew. While fighting to stay alive during a dreadful wind storm called a williwaw, he learns first-hand about God's faithfulness.

*WILLIWAW WINDS* is the perfect book for kids 8–12, for homeschoolers, parents, and grandparents. In fact, it's for almost everyone.

The author is available for speaking engagements on a variety of topics.

—Spiritual Victory Over the Storms (Williwaws) in Your Life

—You're Never Too Old to Start a Home-based Career

—How to Self-Publish Your Stories

—For Kids: How to Write Creatively

—How to Turn Your Experiences Into Fiction

Contact: www.sallybair.com,
        www.cedarhavenbooks.com,
        Sally Bair, c/o Cedar Haven Books,
          P.O. Box 186, Washburn WI 54891, or
        cedarhavenbooks@gmail.com

# Order Form

Please send me _____ copies of *WILLIWAW WINDS*.
I am enclosing $7.95 plus $2.50 postage for each book.
Total Enclosed: $_____

Name: _____

Address: _____

City: _____ State: _____ Zip: _____

Phone: _____

email: _____

Send CHECK or MONEY ORDER ONLY to:
Sally Bair
c/o Cedar Haven Books
P.O. Box 186
Washburn WI 54891

*Williwaw Winds* is also available at bookstores and
online at: www.cedarhavenbooks.com or
www.sallybair.com

Please allow 4 to 6 weeks for delivery.